FIRST MATE'S PET

DRAKE LAMARQUE

GREY KELPIE STUDIO

ISBN 978-0-473-49565-7

Cover by Sarah Loch of Purple Dragon Design

www.purpledragondesign.com

Printed in United States of America via Kindle Direct Publishing

Published by Grey Kelpie Studio

DEDICATION

Dedicated to the founding members of Drake's Crew reader's group.
You are the sweetest, most enabling readers an author could wish for.

CHAPTER ONE - IN WHICH GIDEON RECOUNTS THE RECENT PAST

I reflected, as I woke up in the Captain's bed, warm and content, that I had something of a charmed life. From the moment I set foot on the pirate ship Grey Kelpie, some weeks ago now, my life had become a lot more complicated.

First I had fallen for not just the Captain of the ship, the physically huge and surprisingly sweet Tate as well as the mysterious and dominating First Mate, Ezra. Then I'd been swept off the ship and imprisoned by a murderous sea witch, Solomon. As if that wasn't enough to deal with, I'd met and quickly fell in love with a member of the merfolk, the delightful and curious Ora who helped me escape from Solomon.

And somehow, my lovers and I had all agreed, reunited on the Kelpie, that I didn't have to choose just one lover - I couldn't after all, my heart wanted something from all of them - somehow we'd all agreed to share each other. Or, perhaps they had agreed to share me.

But Solomon had one last trick up his sleeve. Through an agent he had corrupted on the ship, had attacked us once more.

The ship's cat Zeb had been cursed, and after a time of illness had turned into a human form.

And, well, he wanted me too.

In fact, he'd been rather insistent because, in his cat form, he had grown used to sleeping in my bed with me.

And I had gotten myself into the habit of talking to him about all the things that were bothering me, and I had made believe he listened to me. Now, it became apparent that he had listened.

I'm not sure how the magic works, but he remembers all those conversations and thinks of me as "his human".

Well. It took a few days to sort out our sleeping arrangements.

Ezra prefers to sleep alone in his hammock, so I didn't have to worry about him. We set up a net under the bowsprit so that Ora could sleep there in his natural merfolk form. The net allowed him enough of the ocean water to stay damp and he could shift back to his human form to climb in and out.

I wanted to sleep in Tate's bed with him, but Zeb was disgruntled that we weren't sharing the small bed in my cabin. First, I tried to explain that bed was far too small for the both of us when he was in his human form - he was almost six feet tall and broad-shouldered and it was a one man cot. We'd fit in all right when it was just me (a relatively skinny and not that tall man) and him (a literal cat).

But secondly, and perhaps more importantly, that I prefer to snuggle into Tate's side and feel the warmth of his arms around me as I sleep.

"But our bed," Zeb said. He opened his eyes wide and nodded at my cabin. "It's where we sleep."

"Right," I said. "But I would really like to sleep in Tate's cabin because the bed is larger, and Tate is there. I like sleeping beside Tate."

"*Our* bed," Zeb said. He took my hand and kneaded it softly with his own. It was an oddly comforting gesture, and I found myself smiling at him, stretching my fingers out so he could knead at the fleshy part at the base of my thumb.

Tate had appeared, laughing. "There's plenty of room for you, too, Zeb," he said. "If you have to sleep with Gideon so badly, just come in here with us."

Zeb had looked meaningfully at me and tugged my hand towards the cabin.

"You can sleep in there if you like," I said. "That's fine, you have the bed to yourself. But I'll be in Tate's cabin."

For the first couple of nights, we had the same argument over and over, and Zeb would curl up in my cabin, looking comically large as he tucked his legs up, on top of the blanket instead of under it.

Then, every night at around the third hour of the morning, Zeb would push his way into the Captain's cabin and curl up beside me.

It became awkward on the fourth morning. On this morning Tate woke up only enough to pull me in for a hot, sleepy kiss.

I, of course, responded, although I too was in a haze of sleep. The taste of Tate's lips was exhilarating to me, and I instinctively pressed myself against him. We were much of the way towards having sex before Zeb grunted and Tate broke the kiss to look over my shoulder.

"Morning, Zeb," he said sleepily. "You don't mind, do you?"

I felt my cheeks flush. How incredible that I hadn't even felt

Zeb's presence, and had been so close to just... Doing that... In front of him. Practically against him, as he was lying so close.

I half turned as Zeb yawned, his mouth opening wide and displaying his ever so slightly pointed teeth.

"Go ahead," he said, lazily. "I want to see what you do. Mmmm. How you do it."

"Oh good lord," I said, faintly.

"You heard the man," Tate said. He smiled and pulled me on top of him. "Sometimes it's more fun with an observer."

My face was utterly on fire with humiliation, but some part of me responded to what Tate said, as well. There *was* something exciting, an added thrill to knowing that Zeb was watching us. Like I was showing off something - how much Tate and I enjoyed each other perhaps.

Tate gently stretched me open with an oiled finger and when he slipped his finger back out, I slid on top of him with a loud moan. I stroked my hands up his chest and smiled, meeting his eyes as I rocked my hips and took him as deep inside me as I could manage.

Tate gripped my hips with both of his large hands, his fingers pressing into the flesh of my rear, making me jolt and rock my hips even more.

He leaned his head up - tugging on my hips a little for balance - and planted kisses over my chest before sucking my nipple into his mouth. I shuddered with pleasure, panting hard and shoving my hips down harder, enjoying the push and pull of his hands gripping me, the glorious sensation of being utterly filled by him. The press of his hips against my inner thighs and the heat of him below me.

I chanced a glance over to Zeb, who was watching with close interest, his mouth slightly open.

He's seeing us love each other. That shouldn't... that shouldn't make it better, but... it does.

I closed my eyes as Tate shoved his hips against me and I couldn't help but groan louder this time. My body felt made for this somehow, and having Tate so deep inside I felt complete in some way I couldn't understand.

Then, I felt the mattress shift under my knees.

Tate let go of my hip and I opened my eyes to watch him reach out to Zeb, beckoning him closer. Tate fell back against the pillow and grinned.

"Come on, you can help if you like..."

Zeb looked at me and I nodded, humming my approval. Once I was in the midst of a sexual encounter, my inhibitions evaporated somewhat. And lately I had been discovering that the more people were involved, the merrier it was.

Zeb shifted onto his knees and moved against my side, his hands stroking the curve at the base of my spine. He leaned in to lick at my nipple with a slightly rough movement, his tongue seeming to catch on the stiff swell of it. I shuddered bodily and moaned, my hips bucking almost without my intending them too.

The three of us found a rhythm after a few moments of experimenting. Tate showed Zeb how to stroke my cock, and Tate's hand tugged his leather trousers open and stroked him until he was making a curious growling moan sound.

For my part, I slipped my arm around Zeb's shoulders and pulled him in for a kiss, moaning into his mouth as I got close to completion. Zeb ducked his head again and bit down around my nipple, I bucked my hips harder and Tate jolted, filling me with no warning.

Soon enough all three of us were groaning out our pleasure together.

After that encounter, Zeb mostly came to bed with me in Tate's bed, although some nights he seemed to get moody and would choose to sleep alone in my old cabin.

CHAPTER TWO - IN WHICH THE GREY KELPIE ATTACKS

Thirteen days after we had escaped the seas around the Splintered Isles where Solomon, the sea witch, lived, the call went up at midmorning that a likely ship had been spotted.

I was in Tate's cabin, trying to work out the amount of food we needed now that we had lost Joseph but gained Ora and Zeb.

Ora, my merfolk lover, was watching me work. They found paper utterly fascinating and loved to watch me write on it. It was sweet, but a little annoying when they tried to touch the ink before it had fully dried.

They also tried to watch as I wrote in my new journal, a blank ledger book Tate had said I could use, but I had to explain to them it was private and I had trouble writing it with an audience.

But on this day it was columns of numbers and calculations, and Ora was sitting on their hands so as not to be tempted to touch the ink.

Zeb was lounging on the deck just outside the cabin door, basking in the sunshine.

There was a shout - I think it was Shem on lookout - and Tate came thundering down the deck to his cabin. I could always tell when it was Tate's steps, he had no delicacy at all.

"Eh, get out of it," Tate said, grumpily, trying to step around Zeb's sprawled limbs. "You're too big to lie about in doorways now, Zeb."

"Don't care," Zeb yawned.

Tate had to step around him. I watched with interest as he picked his feet up, curious about what was happening and enjoying watching them together.

"Maybe you could change back to cat form for naps?" Tate said testily.

"I don't know if he can," I said.

Zeb didn't reply, just seemed to resettle himself and close his eyes. It remained strange to see a grown man in leather trousers act quite so catlike, but strange was normal for me now, in a way.

I had learned to let a certain amount of oddness wash over me like sunlight and not react to it as I might once have done.

"What's going on?" I asked as Tate made his way into the room.

"Ship sighted, think it's a slaver," Tate said. He went to the wall and took down his grey woollen coat, although it was a hot and sunny day. "We're going to attack it. You lot can all stay in here where it's safe, if you like." He looked between me, Ora and then back at Zeb.

"Attack it?"

"Aye, time for some piracy," Tate said. My blood chilled a little. But he'd said it was a slaver...

"I can fight," Zeb said. He didn't move, and his eyes were still closed.

"Right, uh," I said. I stood up. "No, I'm a part of this ship, I want to help. I don't want to sit quietly shut away in this room like a frightened maiden."

Tate's jaw worked and I wondered if he'd order me to stay put but he nodded instead.

"Very well, you can take one of my spare swords." He opened a large sea chest and pulled out a couple of weapons. "Ora?"

"What's slaver mean?" they asked. They'd been prodding at my workings, blotting it all, and their fingers were black with ink.

"Uh, it's like, men who take other men as property," I said. "Against their will, they're made to work for no money."

Ora pulled a face. "Some of the clans do that with prisoners of war," he said. "I hate it. I will fight. Do you want me to sing?"

"I'm sure that's not necessary," I said, quickly. Tate shook his head at the same moment.

"Just, follow the others," Tate said. He handed us both medium-sized swords and I hefted mine, humiliated at how alien the thing felt in my hand.

I know how to fence, I've been taught. I just haven't practised in a while.

In a long time. That's all.

Zeb stood up slowly, stretching his arms over his head and yawning. He looked at the sword Tate offered him and took it with interest.

"Are- are you sure that's a good idea?" I asked. "He's never used a sword before."

"Something tells me he knows what to do with it," Tate said. He led us back out of the cabin to the deck where the crew had gathered. Ezra, the First Mate, my dark, possessive lover, was stony-faced.

"Slaver all right, recognise the name from the postings I read back in Kingston," Ezra said. "Looks to be a crew of about a dozen, maybe less." The crew of the Grey Kelpie numbered thirteen, which some would think an unlucky number, but to me it was perfect.

"So few?" I asked, and then quickly shut my mouth as it wasn't my place to question him. And it wasn't like we had a huge advantage of numbers to compare.

"Many slave ships run on skeleton staff, once the slaves are chained there's little need for guards," Shem said, grimly.

"Right," Tate raised his voice and looked over to the helm, where Anton was awaiting orders. "Straight on to them, Ant!"

"Aye, captain!"

"The rest of you look alive, I want a few by the longboat in case they try something stupid. Run up the Jolly Roger, let's see if they surrender. Otherwise, this should be a straightforward raid. Watch your backs, watch the backs of the person next to you."

Sagorika came up from her cabin below deck, her skirt hitched up at either hip, a bandolier of knives slung over her chest. Her hair was tied back under a scarf and she looked positively terrifying, her eyes flashing.

I stood there in knee length trousers and a loose white shirt and felt terribly out of place.

"I think I need a more intimidating costume," I said as Sagorika stopped beside me.

"Don't take this the wrong way, sugar," she said. "But you couldn't look intimidating even if you wore everything in Ezra's wardrobe."

"Oh." I tried not to look too crestfallen.

"Ora on the other hand," Sagorika said. She looked past me

and nodded at the merfolk. "Ora looks like they're about to tear someone's throat out."

"I'm probably not going to," Ora said. Ora wore a knee length pair of indigo blue sailor trousers, loose around their thighs, and one of Tate's grey waistcoats. The waistcoat was too big on them, but they somehow made it look like that was exactly how a waistcoat should look. The outfit didn't look intimidating on its own, but Ora was looking serious.

It was such an unusual expression on their face, their eyes became shiny and hard, their cheekbones seemed to jut at an unnaturally sharp angle.

Somehow, even Ora saying they probably weren't going to tear out a throat was chilling. It was the use of 'probably' I suspected.

I swallowed.

Ezra moved closer to me. "You sure you should be out here?" he asked, his voice gruff. "You look even whiter than usual."

I nodded, determined. "Yes, I want to pull my weight for the ship. I want to be a part of this crew."

"All right," Ezra said. "Just try and stay back from the fighting."

He squeezed my shoulder, then went back to Tate's side. I fumed.

"What-what kind of advice is that?" I asked Ora. "I want to pull my weight, and he tells me to stay back from the fighting."

"It would be best if you didn't get killed," Ora said. They turned to look at my face and I saw a flicker of fear in their eyes. "You're too important."

My heart skipped a little. "I'm what? Don't be silly," I said. I shook my head.

"You are, you're valuable to me, to Tate, to Ezra and Zeb," Ora said.

"Me, too," Sagorika added. She patted my shoulder. "I'd be sad if you were skewered. Things on the ship have been a lot more fun since you joined us."

"I like that everyone's assuming that if I were to fight, I'd end up dead," I huffed. "Very nice confidence everyone has in my abilities."

But truth to tell, I didn't have a lot of confidence in my abilities either.

Oh, Mother, what have I gotten myself into? Why is my pride kicking in now of all times? It would be safer in the cabin... but shameful as well.

The Grey Kelpie sped towards its target and I swallowed hard, squeezed the hilt of the sword and tried to remember all the things I'd learned in fencing class.

"No white flag, though they must have seen us," Tate called. "Prepare for battle!"

I wasn't at all ready when Tate ordered for the ship to turn and pull alongside the slaver. I swallowed again, trying to steel myself. I saw the name of the ship, painted on the side. *Stephanie's Tears.*

Tears sounds right, I thought, swallowing the lump in my throat. *How many people's lives have been ruined or lost in your holds?*

I saw Zeb slink through the ranks to Tate's side, he leaned on the ship's railings and hissed.

Then we were properly alongside them, I saw the faces of the Stephanie's crew.

From that moment everything happened very fast.

Shem and the crew threw grappling hooks and tugged the

Grey Kelpie hard against the side of the slaver ship.

The crew of the slaver looked filthy and rough, their beards overgrown, their eyes shadowed. They were trying to cut at the ropes Tate's crew had thrown, but the Kelpie's men were too fast. They hauled on the lines and the deck rocked as the ships bumped against one another.

With the ropes tied off the men swarmed over onto the Stephanie, and our crew was soon locked in hand to hand combat with the slavers.

I hauled myself over the side of the ships where they were hard abutted to each other, lashed with ropes, at the same time as Ora and Sagorika. I breathed fast as the air filled with the smoke and smell of flintlock pistols.

I caught sight of Tate, laying waste to the men around him with a sure hand and a blank expression. His eyebrows were drawn together against the harsh sunlight.

"Behind you," Ora said, and pressed their back to mine as two of the slaver's crew advanced on us. Ora's presence at my back gave me the confidence I needed to raise my sword and glare at my opponent.

He was a tall man with broad shoulders, although not as impressive looking as Tate or Ezra. His face contracted in a cruel grimace, showing all his teeth.

Our swords clashed with a ring of steel, and the impact of it juddered down my arms and through my bones.

I spun away, not wanting him to bear down on me with his strength, which I was sure would be superior. I had to use my size and my speed to gain the advantage, no easy feat on a ship at sea that was crowded with others doing the same thing.

I dodged back as he jabbed at me, then came at him from the side he left open with a thrust. He parried with a knife in his left hand and I flicked my hair back out of my eyes. I thought I had tied it back, but clearly not securely enough.

He brought his sword down towards my head and I blocked it on muscle memory, gasping as the impact jarred my skeleton again.

"This cargo's too precious," he hissed. "You'll kill us all or we'll kill you, no other way out of it now, boy."

I didn't bother to reply. It had been a habit of some of the boys at my preparatory school to do this, try to weaken their opponent with jibes and insults. I had always found my energy better spent on the fight itself.

He pulled back and we circled each other for three steps, and he thrust again. His shoulder gave away his intentions though, and I was able to slip my sword inside his guard and disarm him with a neat flick of the wrist.

I'm remembering more of this than I'd expected. As if my muscles remember the movements.

He gasped, lunged after his sword, and I kicked the back of his knee, sending him sprawling. I placed the tip of my sword at his throat and he froze, looking up at me.

But I hesitated. I didn't want to spill this man's blood. Then I'd have killed him. I'd never killed anyone before.

There was a blow to my side, someone shoved me sideways and I stumbled, almost dropping my sword as I tried to keep my feet. I spun to face whoever had shoved into me - hadn't Ora been behind me? What had happened to Ora?

I couldn't spare a moment to look for them.

The man who had shoved me was already thrusting and I parried it at the last moment. He advanced and I retreated - my heart pounding louder than anything else I could hear on the battlefield.

I kept my eyes on his sword and his shoulder.

Left parry. High block. Keep retreating, this man has a powerful thrust.

Christ, that one nearly had me.

Focus, Gideon, breathe.

Calm is better for fighting.

There - an opening!

Fast as I could manage, I thrust my sword into the gap in his guard and managed to graze his side before he knocked my sword aside with a quick riposte.

I swallowed, feeling a chill of fear. Now he was angry and I was quickly tiring. My arm ached from the weight of the sword and I was having trouble catching my breath.

The man grinned in a nasty way, I think he could tell I was struggling because he straightened his back and barked out a laugh.

"Didn't expect you to have even this much fight in you," he said, advancing. "But I can see I may as well put you out of your misery." I swallowed and planted my feet, readying myself to block whatever attack he had planned.

But I can't win from blocking, I have to attack. I have to defeat him, not just fend off his attacks.

"Get back!"

The voice was a familiar snarl - Ezra - and I immediately jumped back, colliding with the side of the ship but managing to just keep my feet.

In a blur of black Ezra moved between me and the slaver. Before he registered what had happened, Ezra had run him through.

The man fell to the deck with a heavy thud, blood quickly

pooling below him, and Ezra spun and skewered another slaver who was rushing him.

"Oh," I managed to gasp, pulling my hair back from my face and wiping my forehead.

I scanned the deck, and saw the slavers were quickly being overwhelmed by the crew of the Kelpie.

Ora straddled the body of a fallen slaver, their head bent down over the neck in a curiously intimate way, and for a moment I thought they were kissing. But then I saw the blood dripping down the side of the slaver's head and to the deck.

I quickly looked away - where was Tate? Zeb?

"Last chance to surrender," Tate's voice boomed over the deck and I looked aft to see him run a man through and then shove his body overboard.

There was no response. I looked to starboard and saw the last of the slavers fall under Zeb's sword.

Zeb had none of the finesse that Ezra displayed, but a frightening ferocity to his blows. He hissed. His teeth, which were bared, looked pointier than usual, almost fang-like. And when he whirled to look over at Tate I saw a long black tail sticking out of the rear of his leather pants.

"Oh stars," I said, feeling faint.

A tail. He has a tail. He doesn't usually have a tail, why does he have a tail now?

"That's the last of them, Captain!" Ezra called to him. He moved closer to me and squeezed my arm. "You all right?"

I nodded and sucked in a deep breath, trying to will my heart to slow itself.

"Could be some below." Tate strode up the deck, looked both of us over and nodded once. "Come on, time to free some slaves and find out how much gold this ship was carrying."

Ezra and Tate headed below, and I wanted to go after them but I was still trembling from the battle. The air was rank with the smell of spilled blood, and my stomach turned with it. The smell down there would be even worse.

I hadn't been able to deliver the killing blow, and if it hadn't been for Ezra I could have died. I could have lost Ezra, if he'd made one wrong step. Or Tate, come to that. Or any of them.

I looked over to Ora, wanting some comfort, but then I remembered the blood and quickly looked away again.

I knew what they were. I knew they would eat flesh of humans, they told me this. Just ones that would have died anyway and that was certainly the case here.

Zeb trotted over to me, looking pleased. I raised my eyebrows as he bent and sort of bashed his head against my shoulder. It wasn't unpleasant, like the soft headbutts he'd have given me in cat form if he was feeling particularly affectionate.

"Did you see what I did?" He asked. "Wasn't I impressive?"

"Yes, yes, you were, utterly impressive," I said. Since it seemed to be the thing to do, I raised my hand and rubbed it through his hair, startling a little to find two black pointed ears sticking up out of his wild locks. I hadn't seen them at a distance.

Zeb purred, which was a strange but alluring noise from the full-grown man.

"Very impressive indeed."

He purred louder and I felt myself breathing easier.

Impulsively, I wrapped my arms around Zeb's neck and pressed myself against him. After a moment's hesitation, he hugged me back and I breathed in the sweaty, musky scent of him and felt a little more steady.

From below deck came the sound of voices, cheering.

CHAPTER THREE - IN WHICH COMFORT IS SOUGHT

*I*t was a few hours before we were sailing away from the Stephanie.

Tate and the Kelpie's crew freed the slaves, gave them command of the ship and ensured they had food and water provisions, and a map to the nearest safe port. And some knowledge of how to sail the ship.

As for the Kelpie, the slavers's coffers were confiscated and examined.

I was employed to count the gold coins and make some calculations as to how much we would leave but, as I told Tate, the coffers were stuffed with so many riches we could afford to be quite generous to them and still come out with a lot of money to share with our crew.

I related this to him in the unfamiliar cabin of the *Stephanie*. It was none too clean, and I was trying to pretend I couldn't smell anything at all.

"That's excellent news," Tate said. He thumped me heartily on the back, causing me to slam my ribs painfully on the edge of the desk.

I rubbed my ribs and straightened up. "Yes, quite. I had no idea they'd be carrying this much."

Tate grimaced and nodded. "A lot of money in this business, but people don't realise what a toll it makes on the soul."

"I suppose not," I said.

I had gone below deck to see the state of the hold the slaves were kept in and had been utterly horrified. The smell was terrible, unwashed bodies, waste and the mustiness making it worse again. Even now the crew of the Kelpie were helping the freed men and women to clean it out with brooms and buckets of sea water.

"Leave them ten per cent," Tate said. "Once the crew are done below we can make sail."

I still wasn't entirely sure how I felt about the killings, and the thievery. I felt uneasy, for sure, as it was so unusual. But another part of me was so disgusted by what the slavers had been doing it felt like we had only done good that day.

Later, as the sun was beginning to set, the Kelpie set sail, headed for one of the ports on the trade route that Tate said was safe. Tate had told them they were welcome to follow us to the port and see what was what, but the freed folks had been a little weary of us even after the rescue.

And who could blame them?

The Stephanie had maps and compasses, and a few of the folks seemed to have a plan they obviously weren't going to tell us.

The Kelpie's crew were happy with the knowledge that the day had been profitable and maybe a hundred souls had been freed from a terrible life of drudgery and imprisonment.

The atmosphere over dinner was festive.

Despite it all, I felt unsettled still. I wasn't hungry for much of dinner. Tate and I ate at the table in his cabin, and usually Ora and Zeb and Ezra joined us. But tonight Zeb had gone to bed soon after getting back on the Kelpie - in my cabin, on my old bed, of course.

Ora had gone for a swim after the fight and hadn't yet returned. Ezra had wanted to eat with the crew.

I felt a yawning hole in my chest and had no idea how to fix it.

"You all right, Gid?" Tate asked, after I had torn my bread roll into small pieces and eaten perhaps three of the bits.

I nodded and shrugged.

"What is it?" he lowered his voice and peered into my face, I dropped my eyes.

"I don't know, I simply feel..." I cleared my throat. I didn't want to tell him I felt a yawning hole in my chest, that would worry him unnecessarily. "I feel melancholy," I said instead.

"Melancholy?"

"It means sad," I said.

"I know what it means, lad," Tate said. "You may not know this about me but I did actually go to school at one point."

I flushed. "I'm so sorry, Captain, I didn't mean to imply that I thought you were-" I stopped when his finger pressed against my lips.

"You've been calling me Tate," he said. "You should keep doing that. And you have a tendency to get all overly formal and polite when you're flustered, so how about, instead of doing all that, you tell me what it is that's making you *melancholy*?"

He took his finger off my lips and gave me an encouraging smile.

My breath caught a little, because even through the tumult of emotions churning through me, Tate's eyes sparkled and the warmth of his grin still made my heart skip.

I swallowed, wondering what to say. "I suppose... I feel ashamed of myself," I said. "In the battle, I couldn't deliver the killing blow. Everyone around me was..." I paused, battling with the different emotions.

I'd been afraid, ashamed of myself yes, and more than that. Afraid of Ora, for a moment, repulsed by them, which I never wanted to be. I was pathetic, Ezra had to save me from a battle I didn't have the heart to win. Ashamed I let Tate down.

"Everyone around me was doing their part and winning the battle. I let you down." I felt my eyes well with tears, and aghast, I sniffed and rubbed my hands over my eyes. I hadn't expected to cry over it.

My father's voice spoke inside my head. *You're pathetic. Weak, a disgrace. A milksop with too many emotions.*

"You didn't let me down," Tate said. He turned in his seat, moving his knees either side of mine and taking my hands in his. "Didn't I suggest you stay behind in the first place?"

"That's even worse! That means you didn't think I could handle anything. I really am pathetic."

"I gave you the option of not participating in a pirate raid," Tate said. "Last time we talked about piracy you weren't exactly an advocate of the trade."

I pulled my hands away from his to close my eyes and rub my hands over my face. Maybe I could hide from the whole world?

"Hey, now." Tate murmured. He moved closer in and put his arms around me.

I didn't take my hands off my face, but I leaned into his chest. He was just so big and warm, it made me feel a little better.

And his words were comforting, too. I didn't think he'd lie to me, not about this. His tone was so sincere.

Behind us I heard the cabin door open and I startled back from Tate, trying to pull out of his arms, as if it were my Father walking in on us. His voice in my head had made him feel close, like I was back at home somehow.

Tate loosened his hold but didn't let go. "Ora," he said. "There you are."

"Ora..." I breathed.

"What's going on?" Ora asked. I turned in Tate's arms and reached a hand out to Ora. Their naturally curly dark hair was damp, clinging to their forehead and they brought the smell of the sea into the cabin with them. They wore a skirt and nothing else - Ora had never really understood human clothes, but wore them at my request.

Ora took my hand without question and stood behind me.

"Gideon's a little shaken by the battle," Tate said.

"It's not exactly that," I said.

Ora crouched and wrapped their arms around my waist, pressing their chest and cheek to my back. They were chilled cool from the ocean, and I realised how hot and damp I felt. Tate smiled and kissed me gently.

Between the two of them I felt warmth slowly spread through the hole in my chest. Maybe it wouldn't fill it up entirely, but it was definitely a salve.

They both held me for a little while, and then Ora straightened and kissed the top of my head. Tate sat back to finish eating his dinner. I looked at mine and forced myself to eat a mouthful of fish.

I didn't know if anything had been solved, exactly, but I felt better enough.

We made port a day later in a tiny town on the West coast of Hispaniola - aside from a rickety wooden mooring there were a handful of buildings and some market stalls and fishing boats.

"You two stay on board," Tate said to Ora and myself before we moored. We were out on the deck watching the island grow bigger as the ship sailed in, leaning on the rails and wondering aloud what kind of town it was. "This is a small pirate town, and people will leave me alone, but you two, I don't know. Safest for you to stay aboard."

"But I wanted to see all the people living together!" Ora protested. I put my hand on Ora's back and rubbed a circle.

"You can do that in Tortuga, our next port. This is a news and supplies run only. Ezra and I will handle it and we'll set sail again within an hour. Understood?" Tate raised his eyebrows at both of us.

"Yes, we understand," I said quickly. I slipped my arm around Ora and pulled them against me. "We can find something else to do to pass the time."

Tate nodded at the two of us then called to the rest of the crew. "Sagorika, come with us. Shem, you have command while I'm gone. Don't expect anything will happen, though."

"Aye, Captain," Shem said.

"Where's Zeb?" Ezra asked, looking around. I'd last seen Zeb stretched out on the deck near the helm. I looked that way but he wasn't there.

"Up there," Ora said, pointing to the tallest mast.

Up on one of the yards, Zeb was sprawled out asleep. His torso on the wood of the spar, one arm dangling down.

"Oh my god," I breathed. One wrong move and he'd plunge to the deck. "He's going to die."

"He's a cat," Ezra said. "He'll have the best balance out of anyone on the ship."

Tate nodded and squeezed my shoulder. "Don't worry about him, back when he was a cat, he did like to be high up in the air. I'm sure it's the same now."

"Right," I said, softly. I pulled my eyes away from Zeb's sleeping form. The idea of being that high up terrified me even though I stood with my feet on the deck.

Ora slipped their arms around me and I leaned against them.

"Right, let's get to the market and get this damned errand over with," Tate said. He patted his belt where a fat pouch of coins hung, checked his sword and nodded to me and Ora. "Back soon."

Tate strode down the gangplank, followed by Ezra and Sagorika. The three of them looked every inch the kind of pirate I would have been terrified to meet on a dark night, back in Kingston.

Terrified and a little excited.

Although I worried for their safety, I didn't worry too much. Anyone who thought to interfere with their business was surely going to get the worse of it.

Ora turned towards me and pouted a little. "What are we going to do instead of seeing the town?"

I had been about to suggest something utterly salacious, but looking into their face, my memory supplied an unwelcome image: Ora, head bent over the neck of a dead or dying slaver, blood flowing onto the deck. I swallowed hard.

Ora's eyebrows drew together. "What's wrong?" they said. "You smell... afraid?"

"I'm not afraid of you, exactly," I said. "I just... when you attacked that slaver the other day, you... that scared me. I didn't expect to ever see you do something like that."

"I'd never hurt you," they said. They took my hand in theirs and kissed my fingertips gently.

"I know that. You're one of the most gentle beings I've ever met," I said. "To me. I just, I can't forget it."

Ora's face fell and my heart twisted. I hated making them feel bad in any way. I cleared my throat and squeezed their hand with mine. "Maybe you can replace that memory with something else?"

Ora smiled, their whole face lighting up with it, and they tugged me towards Tate's cabin.

It was a comfort that their teeth weren't pointed.

In Tate's cabin, Ora unbuttoned my shirt with somewhat clumsy fingers and I stroked my hands over their bare chest.

"This is all still so new," Ora said, softly. "I like the way it makes you look, but I also like how you look without it."

"I like the-" Ora kissed me, their lips cool and familiar.

I keep on feeling as if I already knew you, I thought. But I was afraid to say those words aloud. Perhaps it was simply the idea of a soulmate, although I wasn't at all sure if merfolk had souls, or if soulmates were a real thing.

"Quiet," Ora said, breaking the kiss. "Let me take care of you, you don't have to say anything."

"Mm, that sounds nice."

"*Quiet,*" Ora hummed a little and drew me to the bed, their hands loosening my trousers and I tugging their skirt open. "Let me do it."

I nodded, biting my lower lip through a smile, not speaking would be a challenge at the start but I often lost control of my words once I was in the midst of pleasure.

Ora lay me on my back on the bed and draped themself over me.

They reached up to stroke my hair back from my face - I had taken to wearing it loose around my shoulders lately, rather than tied back. Unless I needed it out of the way. They carded their fingers through my hair and tugged gently, making me hum softly.

Ora was usually gentle with me, but this time they were being intentionally even more careful. They wiggled their hips and slid our cocks together, causing us both to moan.

Sitting up and letting their fingers trail out of my hair, they stroked their hands over my chest, teasing at my nipples until I was breathing heavily. My hips, quite of their own accord, rocked against Ora's rear where he sat straddling me.

"I..." I started, but Ora leaned in and kissed me quiet, their tongue pushing between my lips to tangle with mine.

I didn't need another reminder to be quiet - Ora knew what they were doing.

I moved my hands up their thighs and caressed their hips, wanting to give back a fraction of the gentle pressure they were already giving me.

Ora smiled, dipped their head down to kiss at my neck. My body shivered deliciously and I rocked my hips against them again.

I slipped a hand behind to start stretching Ora open, and felt them breath hot air, damp against the skin of my neck and then gently bite down on my skin.

I froze for a moment - *Ora drinking blood or... eating flesh?*- but it was gentle, they would never hurt me. I relaxed and wrapped my arm around their waist, my other hand dipping inside to feel Ora's naturally occurring slickness.

"You're safe with me," Ora murmured into the skin below my ear and I closed my eyes, letting my head tip back and offer them more access to my throat.

"I know, love."

I scissored my fingers and Ora moaned softly, then lifted their hips to sink down on my cock. Both of us shuddered with the feel of the heat of me filling them. Of being so intimately connected.

Ora kissed a trail from the hollow of my neck, up over my Adam's apple and under my jaw until they were kissing me again. Harder this time but with love and passion.

They sank all the way down and I groaned into their mouth. Seized with a sudden need to touch them everywhere, I ran my hands over their torso, back, sides, wanting so much to possess and give at the same time.

"Uh uh." Gently, Ora caught my hands in theirs and brought them to their mouth. They kissed my fingers and then gently bit them, causing electric jolts of pleasure to shudder through me and into Ora. They placed one of my hands on their hip, pressing over the back of my hand to encourage me to leave it there. The other they continued to mouth at as they started to rock their hips in earnest.

I dug my fingers as gently as I could into Ora's hip and choked on a gasp, opening my eyes to watch as Ora rode my cock. It was absolutely obscene, my fingers in their mouth, their lips slack, their eyes half closed and pitch dark. Their eyelashes thick, feathering their cheeks with each blink.

Their chest pushed out as they arched their back and rode me faster, panting around my fingers.

I moved my hand from their hip to their cock as I started to push against them, driven by the need building inside me. I stroked them slowly, a counterpoint to the increasing speed of my hips.

Ora whimpered deep in their throat, letting my hand fall from their mouth finally, so I rubbed at their nipple.

They were bouncing on their knees now, pulling up and slamming down on me with enthusiasm, as I pushed my heels against the bed and shoved up into them, gasping with the consuming heat of it.

My hand pumped their cock faster and soon they were spilling over my fingers and stomach, I cried out and filled them with my own seed.

Both of us panting, Ora fell forward and crashed their mouth against mine for the most wild, carefree kiss we'd ever shared. I returned it enthusiastically.

I wrapped my arms tight around them and we kissed and kissed. Tangled up in each other we spent the next hour petting, kissing and rolling our hips together to make each other moan. The world had melted away and it was just the two of us, lost in giving each other pleasure.

Because I found, the more I touched Ora, the more I felt. Their moans spurred mine on, the fact of them getting aroused incensing my own arousal more. It was a magical, sensual thing that left me thirsty and wanting more.

Eventually, I heard Tate's voice, it was louder than normal. "If we're quick we can catch the wind, I'm taking the helm!"

"That doesn't sound good," I said. I got up out of bed and pulled on my trousers, grabbing my shirt off the back of a chair where it had landed.

Ora followed a little slower, pulling on a skirt and nothing else.

I stepped out of the cabin and blinked in the sudden bright sunlight.

Ezra was pulling the mooring lines in, so I approached him first. "What's going on?"

"Navy nearby," Ezra grunted. "Tate's taking us straight to Tortuga to avoid them."

"Tortuga?" I had heard stories of what happened in Tortuga - long debauched parties, mayhem in the streets, no laws. Of course, I had no idea if that was true.

"Aye," Ezra turned and gave me a wicked, wolfish smile. "In Tortuga, you and I are going to have alone time, Gideon."

I felt a jolt flash through my body, starting somewhere around the base of my skull and ending in my cock. My fingers tingled. "A-alone time?"

Ora chuckled and draped an arm around my shoulders.

"There's a place I plan on taking you, get you... outfitted."

Ezra looked me up and down, his eyes lingering around my crotch, chest and neck, and I felt as if I hadn't put clothes on at all. Well, Ezra knew what I looked like naked, after all. He was probably imagining it all very clearly.

"Outfitted?" I repeated, stupidly. I closed my eyes and shook my head, Ezra was making me flustered and I had no idea what he was talking about.

"He's teasing you," Ora murmured in my ear. I felt my skin tingle. Ora sounded amused. They kissed my cheek, let go and waved at Ezra. "I'll leave you to it."

Ezra nodded at Ora and moved closer to me. Close enough to touch, but he made no move to do so. I instinctively knew not to touch him myself.

"What we shared, back in the brig, that was a taster. Just a tiny little bit of the sort of things I can do to you. Understand?"

My breath was fast. Of course, I remembered every second of being in the brig with Ezra - or rather, just outside it - he'd bound my hands and teased me, before fucking me so hard and so good I'd thought about it every night since, even if just for a moment. I wanted to know how far he'd go with binding me, or what it really meant to be his pet as he'd called me.

I felt on the edge of something divinely sinful and I wasn't sure what to expect from his promises, but I wanted them all the same.

"I..." I wasn't sure what to say to him at all. "I don't know that I do understand."

"Well." Ezra lifted a hand and touched his fingers to my jaw, then slid them back under my ear to caress the back of my head. "You will learn what it is to obey, and how much pleasure and pain you can take. That's all I'll say for now, and you can let your imagination go wild."

I'd forgotten how to breathe.

I was close to just begging him to take me then and there, but it was broad daylight on the deck of the ship. There was crew everywhere, and I knew Ezra. He *wanted* this to be something that ate away at me.

He wanted to see me wondering and agonising over it. He was going to enjoy that?

Leaning in, Ezra planted the softest of kisses on my lips. Another tease.

I whimpered in the back of my throat, closing my eyes and wishing for more but knowing there was no chance I'd get it.

Why does that make it all the more appealing? I had never thought that being denied something would make me want it so much more intensely. As if he's set kindling inside me and lit it, but there's nothing like a proper flame yet.

"Understand now?" he growled, pulling back from the kiss but twisting his hand in my hair.

"Yes," I said.

"One night until Tortuga, maybe two, depending on the wind," Ezra said. He let go of my hair and I sucked in a much needed breath.

"Right, good," I said. I nodded. My mind blanked and as ever, I fell back on the manners I'd been taught in school. "Thank you for your time."

I flushed red again as Ezra laughed, mocking me. He ruffled his hand through my hair and went back to coiling ropes. Seeing him handling rope sent another flush of anticipation through me.

"You're such a strange one, Gideon."

"Yes, quite."

CHAPTER FOUR - IN WHICH THE FUTURE IS CONSIDERED

*T*ate cut a fine figure at the ship's helm. His long naturally wavy hair flowing over his shoulders, his eyes bright and sparkling green in his tanned face.

His shoulders broad, seeming to strain the fabric of his white shirt, which he wore half open, showing off his gorgeously muscled chest.

Evidently I wasn't entirely worn out by Ora, I thought as my mouth watered, looking at Tate. Ezra's teasing had me on edge, ready to jump or possibly, jump into bed.

"Hello, Gid," Tate said. "Ezra caught you up on the plans?"

"Sort of," I said. "Mostly he teased me."

Tate laughed - not unkindly - and let go of the wheel to put an arm around me. "Poor Gideon. I take it you and Ora entertained yourselves while we were ashore?"

"Well, yes," I said. I pressed against his side, trying to put my arm around his waist but finding I couldn't reach as well as I wanted to.

Tate chuckled again and kissed the top of my head. "News

has it your father's ships are near, and that they're looking for you."

My blood chilled then.

My father. I didn't want to think about him. Not when I had made this life for myself on the Kelpie.

Tate squeezed me closer against him. "Which is why we're making haste for Tortuga. There's no love for the Navy in that port, and we can lose them, hopefully. And hopefully they don't even know you're on this ship, but... they say they're around. Searching."

"I don't want to go back," I whispered.

"I know, lad, and the stars know I don't want you to leave the ship either. Besides that, if the Royal fleet catches us they'll hang Ezra and me for sure. The others, well... Who knows. Gaol or the noose."

I didn't want that image in my head, but it was conjured all the same with Tate's words. Tate and Ezra side by side, legs hanging limply, never to move or speak again. I closed my eyes and shuddered.

"I'll never let that happen to you," I said.

"That's admirable, lad, but I don't think you can hold them off if they attack. Our best plan is to avoid them."

I sighed, pressing my head against his chest. "Is it possible to avoid them forever?"

"Well, we can try." He stroked his hand over my back and then let go to haul the helm around. The ship was speeding over the waves, and the small port we'd stopped in was in the distance. We were skirting the coastline of Hispaniola, headed for Haiti, and I found myself searching the horizon for the sails of another ship. Where was the Navy? Were they just past the horizon, waiting for us to sail right into a trap?

There was a thump on the deck, I started violently and spun around. Somehow convinced I had summoned the navy to us and they had already boarded the ship.

Zeb stood beside me. He'd landed on his feet.

I looked up at him. "Weren't you up the rigging just before?" I asked, my voice faint.

Zeb shrugged. "Yeah."

Tate and I exchanged a concerned glance. "And you just jumped down, just now, and landed fine?"

"Of course."

There was nothing I could say to that. Zeb stretched his arms in front of him then up over his head and moved close to me. Bending a little, he butted his head against my shoulder again.

"You had ears the other day," I said, remembering. I put my hand up to stroke his hair.

"Well, of course he had ears," Tate said.

"No, cat ears, in your human form." I swallowed. "I'm sure I didn't imagine it, and a tail, too..."

Zeb shrugged. "It's better for balance." He moved to Tate and rubbed his cheek on his shoulder. Tate looked bemused at this.

"So, you're saying you grew a tail because you can balance better?" Tate asked. He shrugged under Zeb's cheek and he moved back, looking affronted.

"Of course. It's a wonder you don't do it yourselves." Zeb yawned and looked around, spotted Ora and trotted off in their direction.

"I don't know what to say about that," I said. Tate looked at me and chuckled.

"Not much to say, really." He reached over and tugged at a lock of my hair. "It's magic we don't understand and without the help of a powerful magician we won't be able to. Best not to poke it too hard, and hope things stay as settled as they have been with him."

He checked his compass then called to Shem to take over the helm.

"Keep the course for Tortuga, the wind's good." He said, as Shem trotted up to us.

"Aye, Tate," Shem said. He nodded at me and Tate took my elbow, leading me to his cabin.

"We should talk. Serious, like."

My stomach dropped unpleasantly. I couldn't think of anything good that we could possibly talk about that would be considered serious. Only the Navy or, possibly, the frankly ridiculous number of lovers I was involved with.

Once in the cabin, Tate sat at his desk and I wrung my hands until he nodded for me to sit opposite him.

"We need to talk about the future," he said.

"I thought the plan was to lay low." I shifted in my seat. "Surely the Navy have better things to do than spend their whole time hunting us."

"Aye, as a whole, they do, but your father is angry and I believe he will pursue you."

"It's hard to imagine him caring enough about me to pursue," I said, looking away. My gaze landed on the bed where I had enjoyed so many pleasures. I couldn't imagine what my father would say, or do, if he knew about any of that. He'd probably have me shot. The shame of it all, it would ruin his reputation if it were to become known.

Beside the bed was a low table with a couple of my romance stories stacked on it. Tate had really been enjoying them. Father hated my reading those stories too.

Tate gazed at me for a moment and frowned. "You're his only

child, are you not? He must care for you."

"It will be his honour that's hurting, not his heart." I said distantly, without thinking, and then realised how harsh that sounded. "That's a terrible thing to say about anyone, I'm sorry."

"No, don't apologise. You know him better than anyone," Tate said. "And to be frank with you, it's good information to have. If it's not you so much as his reputation he's worried about it could work in our favour."

"How do you mean?" I leaned my elbow on his desk and leaned my temple on my hand. My head had begun to throb, thoughts of Father were always stressful. I didn't like to think too much about my old life in Kingston or how Father must be working to find me.

"I mean, rather than just hide, maybe there's some kind of scheme or strategy we could use."

I narrowed my eyes at Tate. "Strategy?"

"Well," Tate said. He stood up from the desk and began pacing the room, which didn't take him long with the length of his stride. "Something like... perhaps we fake your death somehow. Then he'd stop looking for you, and you could live free."

I frowned, trying to imagine it. "He'd want to see my body though," I said. "Have a funeral and all. Probably bury me beside my mother..."

"Plenty of young men are lost at sea," Tate said. "I'm sure he'd be contented with some bauble or memento of yours."

"I'm not sure." I chewed my lip.

Tate huffed. "All right, how about... Now, this one will sound a little unlikely, but hear me out. How about we ransom you to him? Get a nice big payout for your safe return." I began to protest but he raised his hand in a quelling gesture and I subsided. "And then, a couple of weeks after you've been returned, when he's satisfied you're alive and well, we fake your death."

"We'd still have the problem of the body and the grave." I said.

"What if we ransomed you, returned you and then stole you away in the middle of the night?"

It wasn't exactly that the idea had merit, because I could think of a number of reasons the plan would fall apart, but the idea of being stolen from my room in the night by Tate, Ezra and Zeb was absolutely titillating.

I flushed red as I imagined it.

Tate grinned wide. "You like that idea?"

"Yes, I, I mean no, I hate the idea. There's so many things that could go wrong! What if you were caught? What if you couldn't find me? What if you were shot before I even knew you were close? And wouldn't he just come after me again?"

Tate waved his hand. "Details, we can work the details out later. But it's a good plan, you see, we'd get the pay out and then we'd get you back."

I felt a little stung at the idea that Tate wanted to be paid for me. Logically, I knew it made sense, money was money after all, and it was a safer way to get it than making war on ships - surely - but it was still very risky.

"I don't like how vulnerable it makes you," I said, instead. "All the people in Kingston would be looking for you after you took the ransom and returned me."

"Well, we could manage that so I wasn't directly involved..."

Tate *really* seemed to like this idea.

I hesitated, I hated to argue with him. He was Captain of the ship after all, and it was possible that Father would pay a substantial sum for me. But then what would he do upon my return? I'd hardly be allowed to wander the port freely as I had before. He'd probably have an eligible girl lined up to marry me the second I returned home and then where would we be?

"There's too many variables," I said, shaking my head.

"But you liked the idea to start with." He came to a stop beside me, leaning back against the desk with his arms folded. His presence was overwhelming sometimes, even though I was largely used to him. He looked over me, one big happy force of nature, his teeth showing and his eyes sparkling - crinkled at the corners.

"I... No, I..." I couldn't meet his eyes for this particular confession. "I liked the idea of you and Ezra coming to steal me from my bedroom in the middle of the night," I mumbled. I felt like I was barely audible but Tate's hand closed on my shoulder and squeezed.

"I see, I'm sure we can arrange something like that for you anyway." He leaned down then, practically folding himself in half as I looked up and we kissed. The kiss was a promise, and the promise was a good one. Tingles shot through me and I felt my bare toes curling into the wooden floor.

Damn it all, now it's both Ezra and Tate who are teasing me with something outrageously obscene and undoubtedly pleasurable. Something that I want so badly I can taste it.

"Yes, quite," I said, keeping my eyes closed so I couldn't see Tate's expression. "In the meantime perhaps we ought to just make landfall in Tortuga and stay there until things blow over a bit?"

"Yes, I think that's the best plan for now," Tate said. He straightened up again and I breathed a little easier. "Tortuga is safe enough."

CHAPTER FIVE - IN WHICH GIDEON ENTERS TORTUGA

$\mathcal{W}$e made exceptionally good time, according to Ezra, and were mooring in Tortuga mid morning the next day. The island itself was a curious humped shape.

"Tortuga means turtle, you see?" Tate said. He sketched out the shape of it with one hand. "That's the shell."

"Oh. Yes, I can see it now," I said. From what I could tell the moorings themselves were in poor repair. The wood ageing and rotting. Unlike in Jamaica, there was no dock master ready to make a record of the ship or take payment for mooring. There were a number of ships already moored, and they all appeared to be pirate or privateer vessels, judging from the flags and customised figureheads I could see.

Zeb paced the deck as we moored.

"What is it? What are you worried about?" I asked him, amused.

"Ladies to see," Zeb said. "Tortuga ladies, they'll be waiting for me."

"Will they perhaps be cats?" Ezra asked, his deep voice amused. "Because you are not any more."

Zeb flashed him a look of annoyance. "I could be. Again. Once I work out how to do it."

"I can probably help with that. Shapeshifting is easy once you've learned, babies have to be taught," Ora said. They'd spent some time that morning preening in front of my looking glass, fixing their curls just so, tugging the shirt they'd borrowed from Sagorika so it sat correctly.

Zeb looked Ora up and down and then nodded, his eyes unreadable. "Yes, later. You will help me. That's good."

Finally the lines were all tied off and the gangplank lowered. Zeb was the first off it, bolting down nimbly on his bare feet.

"Just like when he was a cat," Tate said, shaking his head. He turned to the rest of the crew. "We'll go in shifts, three stay with the ship at all times and keep an eye out for anyone trying to steal it. Use your watch shifts. Ezra, Ora, Gideon and I will have rooms at the Pickled Oyster. Anyone else wants to pay for their own rooms, that's fine with me."

I raised my eyebrows.

That was news, sleeping on land would feel strange to me now, no doubt. The bed wouldn't rock gently on the waves.

"Why would anyone pickle an oyster?" Ora asked me, their nose scrunched up. Ora had only recently tasted a pickled onion and had not cared for it in the least.

"It's the name of a tavern," Tate said. "Come on. You've got all your finery on, let's head out."

I would have liked to be wearing my red brocade coat, but since Ora had taken to swimming around wearing it, the fabric was absolutely ruined. Instead I had my next favourite coat on - an oyster grey silk frock coat over black breeches and a white cravat at my throat. I had tied my hair back in a ponytail with a black ribbon to mark the occasion.

Tortuga may be a pirate port, but at least it was some form of civilisation.

Tate for his part had dressed up as well, and was wearing his cleanest shirt, buttoned up all the way, with this most fetching blue waistcoat over the top. He had then topped it off with a burgundy velvet coat and a pistol bandolier that crossed over his chest. He had brushed his hair out, and waxed his moustache.

Ezra, as ever, was wearing head to toe black, but he seemed to have shined his boots, and he looked a little more refined than usual. He had made his signature pompadour even taller, somehow. The sides of his head were recently shaved. He was bristling with knives and two swords sat on his hips.

Ora wore a long skirt and blouse, and looked absolutely relaxed. I wished I could feel as at ease with things as Ora did, sometimes. They looked less like they were pirate royalty than Tate and Ezra, much more like a young lady out for a garden stroll.

We walked into Tortuga together, the four of us - Zeb was long gone, disappeared into the crowd.

Once we were off the marina and into the town proper the streets were lined with stalls selling wine, ale, hot roast meat and other delicacies.

My mouth watered, longing to taste the local street food, especially since there were several things on offer that I didn't recognise.

However, the people here were nowhere near as clean as the market folks back in Kingston. There were men with no shirts on who didn't appear to ever wash or comb their hair. Many of the women dressed in tight, revealing clothing that announced them as doxies, their faces painted.

There were people of all colours, all races and creeds, and all moving fast as if they had very important business, too many to take in even though I looked all around as we walked.

The streets were uneven, the packed dirt dusty and rutted with potholes and grooves where people walked frequently, and I stumbled once or twice until Ora took my arm to steady me.

On the second floor balcony of a building a woman was wearing a very small top, a shiny red thing which barely covered her chest, and low slung loose pants which meant she was showing a lot of mid-brown skin. She was decked out with golden jewellery on her neck, her arms and even draped over her hair, and she was dancing in a way I'd never seen before. She undulated her body and her arms moved in a serpentine fashion through the air. It was utterly bewitching and scandalous for how scantily dressed she was. I hesitated, slowing down some to watch her.

"Don't tell me you're interested in her," Tate said, grinning at me. I tore my eyes away and shook my head.

"No, I just... have never seen anything like that before." I rubbed my cheek, wishing I didn't blush quite so easily.

"I like her clothes," Ora said. "I wonder if I can get something like that here? Looks comfortable."

I patted my side checking my purse was still there, for it was clear this crowd would be full of pickpockets and thieves. I felt relatively safe walking with Tate and Ezra, but I knew that if any of us were to be targeted by a cutpurse it would be me.

"So many people, so many, and what's that smell?" Ora said. They weren't walking as quickly or as purposefully as the

Captain and First Mate, so I used our linked arms to tug them along.

"Stay close until we're used to the streets," I hissed at Ora, who nodded. But their eyes were wide and they were looking around at the buildings. I was only slightly less awe-struck.

The Pickled Oyster was a raucous place. The building looked to be relatively new, a two storey wooden villa with lots of French style doors opening onto a verandah. The doors all stood open, and the ground floor was cluttered with chairs, tables, and people drinking and eating.

Unlike my imaginings, or the somewhat florid descriptions in my romance novels, this wasn't a place of all-out debauchery. There was no one fornicating on the tables, no barrels of wine with people laid out under the tap, drinking until they nearly drowned.

On the other hand, it wasn't nearly as refined as what I was used to seeing Kingston, the standard of dress was either overdressed pirate fashion - as with Tate, or the bare minimum to be covered. Stained open shirts and unlaced breeches seemed to be the most common mode of dress.

The women were dressed in all manner of clothing. I saw women in pirate style breeches, white shirts and wide brimmed hats, as well armed as Ezra. Women with long, expensive looking ball gowns drinking directly from wine bottles. Women with corsets and skirts hitched up, looking for business.

I swallowed, feeling both overwhelmed and excited to explore.

One of the women with her red skirt hitched up around her hip on one side intercepted our group.

"Ezra," she said. Her arm reached to drape her wrist over his shoulder, pressing her voluminous chest against his. "There you are, baby. You're lucky, I'm free tonight..."

My stomach suddenly had a knot in it as hard as if I'd eaten something that disagreed with me. I tensed and Ora's hand rubbed soothing circles on my forearm.

He delicately removed her hand from him. "Sorry Myra, but I won't be needing your company tonight."

She pouted spectacularly, her lush lips pushing out as she batted her thick eyelashes. I had no doubt that this particular combination had changed the mind of many a man (and possibly woman as well) but Ezra didn't waver.

"But Ezzy, baby, nobody thrashes me like you do, I've missed you..."

Tate coughed, and I glanced at him, sure he was swallowing a laugh. He arranged his face into a sort of mild amused expression.

"Myra, sit back down or go find someone else," Ezra said. His voice was a little less indulgent than it had been.

I felt a thrill of relief as she huffed and folded her arms over her ample chest. "Fine. But you're missing out, and don't come crawling to me if you change your mind."

"I never crawl," Ezra said.

She turned in a flounce of ruffled skirts and disappeared into the building.

"Ah, I think you've lost a friend, Ezzy," Tate said, lightly.

Ezra's shoulders hunched up towards his ears and his head whipped to the side, his eyes shooting daggers at Tate. "Don't you ever, *ever*, call me that. Ever. Captain or no, I will gut you."

Tate laughed and slapped Ezra on the back. "You will not."

"I would."

"You could try," Tate said. "But I think you'd find I'll disarm you before you could."

Despite the venom that had been in Ezra's voice, it felt like they were simply teasing each other, the way friends do. I was struck with how little I knew about their past, how had Ezra joined the ship? How had they cooperated over the years? I resolved to ask them at some point when we were less fully occupied.

Tate led us inside, still laughing some. He went to the bar and booked us some rooms on the upper levels of the villa.

"One for me and Gideon, one for Ezra," he said. He looked at Ora. "You all right doubling with us or Ezra?"

Ezra cleared his throat, although he tolerated Ora, he was still wary of the merfolk's ability to sing magic and his possible tendency to drown and eat people. My heart ached a little, I wanted so much for them to get along with each other.

Ora nodded. "Or I'll swim in the harbour, I don't need to sleep so much."

"Gideon's mine tonight," Ezra growled.

I shivered pleasantly, and Tate raised his eyebrows. Then he nodded, paid the barkeep - a surprisingly slight and short woman with a ragged scar across one of her cheeks.

"You can have the rooms as long as you like, Tate," she said. "We're not so busy at the moment, as you can see."

"Thanks, Nelly," he said. "Had any Naval ships through lately?"

She sputtered a laugh and shook her head, handing him two brass keys."What do you think this is, Port Royal?"

"Glad to hear it," Tate said.

"Upstairs, rooms six and seven, seven's the corner with two

windows. I'm sure I don't have to tell you to put the chain on when you sleep."

I was surprised - the inn's very owner - or manager, whoever she was - was admitting it wasn't safe to sleep there? Maybe the town *was* as rough as I'd initially imagined it was.

Tate checked the keys in his hand and handed Ezra the one with the tag that read six.

"Hot bath for me, please."

"Come on, Gideon," Ezra said. "Let's go shopping."

"Shopping?" I felt like half of my conversations lately were just me repeating things back to whoever I was talking to. It was beginning to be frustrating.

"Yes. Thanks for the room, Tate," Ezra said. "We'll see you at dinner, perhaps."

"Oh, right," I said. "Um, well, see you soon Ora." I kissed Ora's cheek and gave them a quick squeeze. "Tate, will you keep an eye on Ora, just until they understand a bit about the place?"

"Course," Tate said. "Come on, Ora, I'll show you what a hot bath is like."

A twinge of jealousy flashed through my chest - I wanted to be there while Tate and Ora had a bath... I wanted to help Ora to understand.

But Tate gave me an encouraging wink, and I felt Ezra's hand close around my wrist.

"Come on, peacock," Ezra said. "Don't you want to see what I have planned for you?"

Oh Lord, what could it possibly be?

CHAPTER SIX - IN WHICH EZRA OUTFITS GIDEON AT A VERY PARTICULAR STORE

*E*zra led me through the town with his hand around my wrist. There was something comforting about it, I found. Not quite the same as holding hands, or linking arms, but Ezra walking beside me was impressive and intimidating and being connected to him in some way was exhilarating.

People would know that we were together.

Or assumed he had kidnapped me, perhaps?

Either way, I liked the feeling.

Besides, I had no idea what he had planned. Shopping? I had to assume it wasn't going to be clothes shopping.

"Are- are you going to uh, let me know what we're doing?" I asked, looking at him sideways.

Ezra smirked, cut his eyes to me and then looked ahead again. "I don't think I can explain it in a way that will make sense. You need to see this first, but know that it's instrumental for your training."

His hand tightened around my wrist and my fears and uncertainty evaporated a little. I trusted Ezra, and he'd never given me anything that I hadn't thoroughly enjoyed.

"How often have you been to Tortuga?" I asked, wondering about the woman, Myra.

"Hundreds of times," Ezra said.

On the tip of my tongue was another question, but something told me there was no good answer, and probably no reason to actually ask it. It didn't matter how many lovers he'd had before, or what gender they were. The only thing that mattered was what he and I were going to do together.

He turned down an alley and I kept pace with him, looking around with interest. The buildings were largely single story houses or stables. There were signs attached advertising various business and services.

A sign that said *Oracle and Mystic*, caught my attention. It was beautifully painted with a large purple eye and a circle around it. Ezra led me past another inn - this one was called The Singing Swan - and then we stopped at a saddlery.

"Saddles?" I asked. I looked up at Ezra in confusion. I knew he liked to dominate but surely he didn't intend to outfit me with a horse saddle? What could possibly be the appeal of that?

"Not exactly." Ezra gave me a flash of his wolfish grin again and we went into the store.

"Nancy? Ben?" he called into the seemingly empty space.

The whole place smelled rich, the air full of leather and polish. It was a heady scent, and at a lack for what else to do, I looked around. From what I could tell this was high quality merchandise, and I wondered why they were operating from Tortuga and not somewhere on a larger island. Somewhere with more horses.

"Hmm?" A tall blond man emerged from behind a rack of bridles. "Ezra. What are you doing here?" He frowned and wiped his hands off on a canvas apron.

"Ben. I'm here to see the special collection, the uh, the back room one." I looked at Ezra, feeling my eyes widen.

Good God in Heaven. I think that's the first time I've ever heard Ezra sound uncertain. Whatever is in this special collection, it's got him a little unsettled.

"Hm, payment before you leave the store," Ben said. He moved to the back and opened a door in the corner. "I'll send Nancy in to help you out."

There was an odd tension in the air between Ezra and Ben. I wondered what the history between them was. Maybe they'd been lovers too?

Ezra flashed a smile at me as Ben opened the door. "You go through first, Gideon."

I moved past him and into the back room. The room was lined with various combinations of leather straps and pieces of metal. I had no idea what I was looking at. The walls had hooks and shelves, and everything was some form of leather.

Ezra pressed his chest against my back and wrapped an arm around me. "I'm afraid I don't understand," I said. My voice came out small and thin, betraying my nerves.

"It's quite simple really," Ezra rumbled. I felt his voice through my back before I heard it properly. "Obviously, if you don't like the idea, you can say no. But I'd like us to pick you out a collar, and some other things. Probably some cuffs, maybe a harness or two. But we're going to try on a few and see what you like before we make any decisions."

"Cuffs? A collar? A collar like you'd put on a dog?"

"Mmhm," Ezra said. "But for a person. For you. To show that you're mine and that you have a master."

He let go of me and moved to the wall and I stayed frozen in the middle of the room.

How humiliating. Collared like a dog. But if it's so humiliating, why is my body heating up? Why is the idea of it being known somehow that I have a master the most alluring and arousing thing I've heard all day?

"Here, let's start with this one," Ezra said. He pulled a thick black leather collar down from the wall and brought it over to me. My eyes were fixed on it.

"I don't think I can wear something like that," I said, in a small voice.

Ezra cocked an eyebrow. "Just try it, for me, all right? If you hate it we'll move on but I have a sneaking suspicion you won't hate it."

I swallowed and nodded. If it meant so much to Ezra, then I would try it, at least. I fumbled with my cravat and pulled it off, draping it over the back of a chair. I took a little longer removing it than I needed to, trying to put off the moment he'd put the collar on me. Finally I straightened up and faced him again, my cheeks flaring hot.

"Lift your chin for me, pet." His voice was softer now. Perhaps it was his tone more than his words that convinced me to lift my chin and let him put it on me.

The leather was cool against my skin, and surprisingly soft. He wrapped it around my neck, moved behind me and lifted my ponytail aside. I felt the leather tighten as he fastened the buckle at the back of my neck. My fingers came up to touch it where it lay against my skin and I felt the heavy metal ring that was fastened to the front of it. The leather felt smooth and appealing under my finger pads.

"What do you think?" Ezra murmured, leaning in to kiss the skin under my ear. I shivered.

Despite my misgivings, I was getting hard.

I swallowed, felt my Adam's apple bob behind the leather and knew I couldn't deny that it was doing something good for me.

"I think, I think it's uh, fascinating," I stuttered. "More sensual than I thought."

"Good." He gripped me by my shoulders and turned me around. "I'm not sure about this particular one though. It might be a little thick on you..."

"It is?" I touched it again.

He unbuckled the collar and took it away, I felt the chill of the air on my neck where it had been covered previously. Strange how quickly I got used to wearing it.

"Maybe this one." He brought over a slimmer one in a deep brown colour. He buckled it on my neck and stroked his hands over the collar and my neck. "Mm, this suits you better. The big one might be good for Tate, maybe." His voice was low, almost as if he were musing to himself but that image sent a shock of pleasure through me and I swallowed hard.

"I'd... I'd like to see that."

"Then we'll see if we can make it happen."

He set the black collar over a nearby rail and looked me over. "Take off your coat."

I shrugged the coat off and draped it over the chair, rolled my shoulders in anticipation of whatever was coming next.

I became aware of how warm I'd been with a coat and a shirt and a cravat on. My skin was damp from the humidity, and my shirt had begun to cling to me. Perhaps it was simply the closeness of the room we were in, or the subject matter that Ezra was not quite talking about, that also made the situation worse.

When I turned back to Ezra, trying to pull the cotton fabric away from where it clung on my chest, he was holding something large and almost spider-like - at least five black straps held together with silver rings.

"You like fancy things, so this is probably too simple," Ezra said, half to himself. "But it's a starting point."

"What is it?"

"Chest harness," Ezra said. He moved closer and slipped the thing over my head. Two of the straps rested on my shoulders, and came together at a silver ring on my chest. Two more straps hung down, and with quick and practised movements, Ezra connected them to straps at my back. He turned me around and fiddled with buckles that rested on my shoulder blades until the whole thing tightened snugly around my chest and shoulders.

I swallowed, again my hand moved up to touch the leather where it sat comfortably against my chest. It felt strange - confining, but not in any actual restrictive way. Like the collar, it felt like a reminder that at any time I could be bound - or perhaps a reminder that Ezra had a claim on me. A sign of my willingness to submit myself and my body to him.

I know my cheeks were burning as I thought through all of this and Ezra tightened the straps a little more, adjusting until my breath was short.

Thank heavens it's just the two of us in here.

"How does it feel?" Ezra smirked, moving in front of me to look me over with a critical eye.

"Yes, uh, good," I said. Ezra's eyes lingered on the hardening bulge in my breeches and I moved a hand to cover myself. "I like the way it feels."

"Arm binder, maybe," Ezra mumbled, watching me. "But definitely a more complicated harness. This one's too plain on you. Although it would look good on Zeb, I think."

"I don't know that he's into... any of this..." I stuttered. I'd only really had that one encounter with him, after all.

"He wears leather pants," Ezra said, as if this proved his point.

Perhaps it did. I had no idea leather working places had products such as this one at all, perhaps there were all sorts of leather rules and meanings to clothing I didn't know about.

I wondered if saddleries back in England had secret back rooms to cater to people with Ezra's - and my - tastes, but it seemed impossible to believe.

He reached around me to undo the buckles and on impulse I went up on my toes and kissed him on the mouth. Ezra kissed back but distractedly, undeterred from his task of taking the harness off me. There was a quirk to his mouth as he turned away though, something pleased there that made my heart thump.

Ezra pulled another harness off the rack. This one had slimmer straps, and more of them. Several buckles hung down and I swallowed, mouth going dry as he brought it towards me.

Behind me the door opened and I heard footsteps. I tore my eyes from Ezra approaching with more leather and saw a woman with long curly brown hair and a canvas apron over a sensible shift dress. I hurriedly stepped behind the chair with my coat on it to hide the bulge in my trousers.

"Ezra, welcome back," she said. "Been a while. Oh, that looks lovely on you, sweetheart." To my consternation, she lightly tapped the collar on my neck and gave me a smile. "Need some help, do you dear?"

"Nancy," Ezra said. He smiled in a friendly way, which wasn't something I was used to seeing from him. "It's been too long."

She kissed him on the cheek, and he kissed her on her other

cheek. She glanced at what he had in his hands and then nodded. "Yes, that one will look good on his frame, it's quite a sweet, delicate style, don't you think?"

Sweet? Delicate? Me?

I flushed again and cleared my throat. "I don't think that's quite appropriate," I said.

Ezra clicked his tongue against his teeth and shook his head at me once. I bit my lip.

"Now, pet, Nancy's here to help. And let's face it, your frame is delicate, especially compared to mine." He slipped the new harness over my head and I shifted from one foot to the other.

I hadn't minded too much when it was just the two of us but now there's this woman here. Watching and judging and... she knows what we're going to do, she knows why we're looking at buying this paraphernalia.

Oh, stars in Heaven, she knows what my sex life is like. Well, this part of it anyway.

My traitorous body apparently found this just as arousing. I closed my eyes and tried to pretend I wasn't there as Ezra fastened straps, then I felt Nancy's hands helping and had to open my eyes to see what was going on.

This harness had the same shoulder strap coming to a central ring at my chest, but there was a second ring below it. The second ring had more straps, and each strap had a silver ring attached to it.

The harness came together snugly with Ezra pulling at the buckles on my back until my entire chest and half my torso was encased in the leather straps.

"Here, love, take a look at yourself," Nancy said. With her kind tone she instantly put me at ease, and I wondered if it was some sort of misguided longing for my mother.

She led me to a full length mirror I hadn't noticed before near the door we'd come in through. Of course, people would like to see how these things looked before they purchased them.

Looking at myself in the mirror I caught my breath.

"Oh," I said. "I see."

I had never thought of myself as particularly handsome or attractive before. I knew I wasn't ugly, I didn't have my father's bulbous, onion-looking nose for example, and my skin was clear, but I never counted myself as handsome in the way Tate or Ezra were. I felt I had never been masculine enough to look attractive. Too delicate, as they'd said.

But as I looked at myself in my shirtsleeves, a leather collar around my neck and the straps of the harness accentuating the muscles of my chest, I saw what the others must somehow have already seen in me.

I was attractive. Handsome even? I wasn't bulky and strong looking like Tate, or mysterious like Ezra, but perhaps there was something else there.

My eyes dropped to the bulge in my breeches, which was - embarrassingly - still there, and I tried not to think too much on that.

Nancy ignored it completely, for which I silently thanked her.

Ezra moved behind me and slipped his arms around me, fingers playing over the straps around my waist and up my chest. "Mmm, I think this is the one. Do you have it in the same brown as the collar?" He asked, addressing Nancy and not me.

I leaned back against his chest, practically melting at the feel of his fingers over me, combined with the snugness of the leather.

"Of course, love. I expect you'll be wanting some other accessories too?"

"You know I do," Ezra said.

Then they were both undoing the buckles and pulling the harness off me and I felt curiously bereft, as if I'd lost something important.

Nothing to worry about, Ezra's buying it, and then back at the inn, he'll show me the true purpose of all of these things, I'm sure.

I crossed the room as they went to the wall and discussed mysterious things like clips and straps and binders.

I picked up my coat and then realised I still had the collar on. I set the coat down and reached behind me to undo the buckle. It was sort of hard to navigate.

"What are you doing, pet?" Ezra asked. Startled, I looked up to find him directly in front of me with another harness, same as the last but in the same brown as the collar.

"Uh, taking this off, so that you can buy it?" I asked, feeling that I had in some way, done the wrong thing but uncertain of what it was.

"Ah, no, you're wearing it out," he said. "Nancy knows the price. And you'll wear this too."

I looked at the harness in his hand and flushed red again.

"I'll... what? Wear it? But we have to walk through town, people will see..."

"That's the idea," Ezra said. He was enjoying my discomfort, and I saw then that although the items from this store were for me, they would likely bring him the most pleasure.

"But, but Ezra," I stuttered. I couldn't see any way of convincing him out of it, but I had to try. "It's humiliating, and everyone will see and know what we're doing, surely that's dangerous?"

Nancy snorted.

"Pet," Ezra said. He started to put the new harness on me, which frankly, felt like he was being underhanded, because I loved the feel of the leather against me already. "If you really don't like it, then you can ask me to stop. But if you're worried about what others will think, you don't need to. There's nothing we can do on the streets of Tortuga that hasn't already been done, and seen by everyone who lives here at least three times."

I glanced over his shoulder at Nancy, who caught my eye and nodded. "It's true, you know."

So, it'd just be me who's embarrassed? But it would be me, being embarrassed?

But... it's hard to catch my breath, and I'm practically dripping in my breeches, so...it appears I'm actually aroused by this whole idea. And if I please Ezra, surely that's part of this training that he keeps going on about.

Oh dear, I'm about to agree aren't I?

Ezra had put the harness over my shoulders, but was patiently waiting for me to speak before he tightened the straps and fastened the buckles. I swallowed hard, gathered up my strength and met his eyes.

"Yes, all right," I said, although my voice sounded strained. My heart was pounding and I had a little trouble catching my breath.

"That's a good boy." Ezra leaned in and kissed me, soft at first and then becoming hard and passionate and I moaned softly into his mouth.

He pulled back and started fastening buckles around me and I, for my part, tried not to fidget.

Once he was done he kissed me again and I started to feel less worried and more comforted. Ezra would be beside me after all, through this whole thing, and Ezra would never let anything bad happen to me.

"How about these ones?" Nancy said, once Ezra had pulled back.

"Perfect."

"And I'll put the others in a bag for you," she said.

Ezra slipped leather cuffs around my wrists, they were the same matching brown leather and had large metal rings on them. They buckled tight and felt rather comfortable.

"I'll spare you the full parade," Ezra said. "You can put your coat on over that lot, and I won't bind you until we're in private."

"Oh, I-I, uh, thank you?" I asked, somewhat confused.

I went to pull my coat on, tugging the sleeves over the leather cuffs and wrapping my cravat around my neck, checking in the mirror that it covered my collar. There was no hiding the leather straps on my chest though. Either I let the cravat hang down and obscure them, revealing the collar, or I used it to cover the collar and the straps were on display.

While I fussed, Ezra and Nancy handled payment, and I think Ezra picked up some more things, but I tried not to wonder too much about them. My mind was consumed with what was about to happen.

Maybe people will just think I have my belts on wrong?

Why would that be any better?

Wait, why had he said he'd wait to bind me until we were in private. Does that mean that at some point he intends to tie me up in public? And why is that *arousing as well?*

Oh Lord, Ezra had better make this worth the humiliation.

CHAPTER SEVEN - IN WHICH GIDEON BEGINS HIS TRAINING

The walk back through Tortuga to the Picked Oyster seemed to take at least three times as long as the walk to the saddlery had. Ezra carried a canvas sugar sack which clanked every now and then.

He didn't hold my wrist this time, evidently he trusted the leather cuffs on my wrists to remind me of his hand there.

It was working. My mouth was dry, my stomach was full of butterflies, my skin seemed to be extra sensitive to the feel of fabric against it, and my breathing was quick. Each breath seemed to strain my chest against the leather harness and remind me it was there, which in turn caused me to breathe faster.

"You really do look marvellous," Ezra said, once we'd gone half a block. I couldn't bear to look at him, instead I was searching the faces of the people around us. Trying to see their reactions.

One ginger haired woman looked directly at the straps and then at the bulge in my breeches, and I tried to twitch my coat shut around me but it wasn't made to be fastened, it didn't cover me. I felt light headed.

What am I doing? This is utterly indecent. All these people going about their daily business, and here I am parading about like... like what? A degenerate? A whore? Plenty of whores on the island, that's probably a large daily business here.

Oh Lord above, I can never go back to polite society now.

"Relax, Gideon," Ezra said. He moved closer and slipped an arm around my waist. It was difficult to lean against him and walk, but it was worth it to feel the solid realness of him against my side.

I felt my head come back to Earth a little. I took a breath of air, concentrated on the salty smell of it. Tried to enjoy the feel of Ezra beside me, of the straps around my chest. Ezra's hand moved up my back and he plucked at one of the buckles through the fabric of my coat. It tightened over my chest and my breath caught, and to my embarrassment, I moaned a little.

"Nng. You like this, don't you, pet?" he growled into my ear, and then bit my earlobe, and I almost tripped because my eyes closed and my legs forgot how to move forward. Ezra's free hand came up to brace my chest, stopping me from falling.

"Oh Good Lord," I breathed. "How much farther?"

"Just about there," Ezra said. "You know, there are harnesses that go between your legs as well, maybe I should have bought you one of those."

He urged me on and I looked at the ground. It seemed to take all of my concentration to put one foot in front of the other and get back to the inn without falling over. And definitely not imagining what it would feel like if the leather snaked down between my legs as well as across my chest.

Suddenly, I realised that getting back to the inn meant the

possibility of seeing Ora, Tate or even Zeb, and they would all surely notice the leather straps and have something to say about it.

If Tate saw, and said something sexual, I'd probably die. Right on the spot. The arousal and humiliation would kill me.

"Head up, pet," Ezra said. "We're here."

I tipped my head back and looked around the common area, searching for anyone I knew. I saw Myra, who gave us one look and quickly looked away again, fuming.

I scanned the bar but there was no sign of Tate or Ora. Perhaps they were still enjoying having their baths?

Ezra took hold of my elbow. "Come on, it's nearly time for the really fun part," he said.

We went upstairs, Ezra hustling me in front of him and me terribly aware of my rear end in his face as we climbed the stairs.

My excitement was tangled in nervousness but I was internally rejoicing that soon we'd be locked in a private room.

At the top of the stairs I hesitated, looking one way and then the other before I spied the room numbers, painted above each door. "Six, wasn't it?"

"S'right," Ezra said.

I led the way to the door and waited beside it while Ezra unlocked it.

He pushed the door open just as the door to number seven swung out and I caught a glimpse of Tate, his head turned, laughing with someone - presumably Ora.

I didn't even think. I darted into room six before they could see me.

"Hello, Ezra, just back are you?" Tate asked, his voice booming in the corridor. I cringed, half hiding behind the open door.

"Aye, Tate. Gideon's uh, feeling a little shy just now." Ezra's voice had an ironic sort of amusement to it, and I rubbed a hand over my eyes, praying that they would move away without questioning it.

There were some words exchanged I didn't catch - Tate murmuring and Ezra replying at the same level, and then I heard two sets of footsteps retreating up the hallway and relaxed, leaning against the wall.

Ezra walked in, closed the door and locked it and then shrugged his coat off and hung it on a hook on the door. He took his bandoliers and weapons belts off too, hung them over the coat.

I watched, uncertain, as he did this. His every movement seemed slow, measured and graceful. Finally he turned to me and smiled a wicked smile that sent lightning through my blood and directly to my cock.

"Come here, pet."

Almost before I had registered his words I was walking towards him.

"You're going to take off all your clothes," he said. "But leave the leather on."

"But it's over my shirt, I don't see -" I stopped when he raised his eyebrows, he was shaking his head gently from side to side.

"I don't want you to argue with me. In fact, let's lay some rules all right? While you have this collar on..." he crooked a finger and hooked it into the ring on the front of my collar, tugging me towards him another half step. My breath stuttered in my throat.

So that's what that ring is for.

"You don't argue with me. You belong to me, you see? I'm

your master, and you are my pet. You do as you're told without arguing. Do you understand?"

"I. Yes, yes, I understand."

"If you disobey me, you get punished."

"Punished?" my voice cracked. He hadn't let go of my collar, so I couldn't move away, although some part of me wanted to flinch back.

"Mmhm, I'll go easy on you tonight, since it's your first time. But if you disobey or argue or talk back, then you get punished."

He slapped my ass with the flat palm of his hand. I jolted, tugging against his hold on my collar and gasping as I was caught short.

He let go of the collar and nodded at me. "Clothes. Off."

"Right," I said.

"And you should call me Master, or Sir, when you address me." He moved to the bed and sat on the end of it, watching me. The sugar sack of extra things from the saddlery beside him.

I took my coat off, hung it on the hook beside Ezra's coat and then removed my boots and breeches, putting the boots beside a wooden chair and laying my clothing over it. As I bent to take these items off, the straps of the harness strained against my chest and I had to catch my breath again.

I was rock hard, and it was very obvious. I unbuttoned my shirt, my fingers fumbling, trembling with the strength of my desire. I had been hard on and off since we'd first walked into that damned room full of leather straps, and it was beginning to ache in a most delicious way.

It took some careful tugging, and a little sweating, but I managed to slip the shirt off my left arm, then off over the right arm. Feeling rather pleased with myself, I added it to the pile of clothes over the chair and smiled at Ezra.

"Very well done, pet. Now, kneel." He pointed at the floor between his feet.

Inhaling, I approached him and sank to my knees. He caressed my jaw with his hand and I leaned into it, grateful for his touch.

He pulled his trousers open and I licked my lips, anticipating getting to taste him. He tugged me closer with his hand on the back of my neck and I closed my mouth around his cock, grateful that now at least, we were getting to familiar ground. I knew what to do with this, and I licked him enthusiastically.

"That's it, get me nice and hard and wet for you," he murmured, his voice rough with desire.

I did as he said, licking and sucking at him, moaning with the taste of him and the knowledge that I was pleasing him.

He began to throb in my mouth and I leaned in, expecting to feel him complete in my mouth but he slipped a finger inside the collar and pulled me back before he did.

I whimpered, feeling deprived. I licked my tips, tasting the traces of him.

"You're doing very well, but we're not done with preparing you," he said.

"Oh, I see," I said. "Should-should I stand, so you can?"

"You should stand up and put your hands behind your back," he said. He dropped his hand from my collar so I could stand.

As I got to my feet, he pulled the sugar sack open and pulled out some more leather straps and some silver metal chains with rings at either end, and several small padlocks.

"What are those for?" I asked, hesitating before turning around.

"Ways to bind you," he said. "Now turn. And call me Sir, or

Master." He slapped my rear lightly and I turned to face the door, pushing my arms back and clasping my hands together behind me.

"Now remember, if there's anything I'm doing that you don't like, you can tell me to stop," he said. I felt a leather strap slip around my biceps and he cinched it, forcing my chest forward as he fastened the buckle.

"Sir, uh, is it not arguing if I say stop? You said I shouldn't argue when I have the collar on."

"No, it's different. I don't want to hurt you in a way you don't like," Ezra said. "And if things get to be too much, you tell me. Say stop, and I'll stop. Got it?"

"Yes, Sir."

I felt a little better then. Knowing that whatever he did, I could stop it if I didn't like it.

It's almost as if I have the power, even if he's the one tying me up so I can't use my hands or arms... and I'm in a collar like I'm his dog.

His pet.

And damn but that's exciting, even though I'm sure it shouldn't be. Maybe it's because it's so taboo...

I tried to imagine what some of the people I used to see at dinners and garden parties back in my old life would say about something like that, but it was so far removed. And none of those people had been my friends, anyway...

I straightened my back as he pulled my wrists together and I heard the jingle of chain and the click of a padlock.

"There now," he said. "How does that feel?"

He left his hand on my waist, a reassurance that I appreciated as I struggled, or rather, attempted move my arms away, but I was quite thoroughly bound. The leather on my upper arms prevented a large amount of movement. I noticed a looking glass to the side and half turned to look at myself, making sure that I didn't lose Ezra's hand from my hip.

There I was, hopelessly pale skinned, slim and lithe compared to Ezra's hard muscles, and deep brown leather across my chest and torso. My arms pinioned behind me and the cuffs at my wrist linked together with chain and locked tight with an ordinary locking padlock.

I had that same sensation I'd had at the store. I realised that I could, in some lights, be seen as attractive, and in this complication of leather, I was desirable.

The idea of any one of my lovers in such a get up was certainly desirable to me, and the thought of Ezra wanting me like this made me feel coveted.

"That's it, admire yourself, peacock," Ezra chuckled. I let my gaze wander to him in the mirror. He was still fully dressed aside from his cock hanging out. And now I couldn't do anything about that. I was blushing again, but he hadn't given me any other orders, so I admired myself in the mirror again.

Ezra shifted and pulled out a pot of coconut oil. He kicked my legs apart with one of his booted feet and I grunted as I spread my legs, trying not to topple over.

He teased me open quickly, careful not to hurt me but not lingering, which was unusual for Ezra. I wasn't going to complain about it though, I wanted him to hurry and fill me up.

Once I was moaning and dripping fluid from my cock onto the hardwood floor, he deemed me ready. Yanking on the leather of my harness he pulled me around. He stood up and kissed me hard on the mouth, making me groan into his mouth and attempt to press against him.

He gripped me by my hips and directed me onto my front on the bed. I used my legs to turn half over, wanting to watch as he stripped off his shirt, revealing the gorgeously muscled chest and his glorious shearwater tattoo when he turned his back to remove his boots and trousers.

I want to lick every inch of that tattoo someday. I want to lick him all over...

I lay trembling, waiting for him, unable to do much except try and control my breathing and watch as he removed the last of his clothes and slicked up his cock with one oiled hand.

"You want this, pet?" He growled.

His eyes were hooded, dark, and he moved closer to the edge of the bed.

Teasing me still... Even though I'm salivating and practically vibrating with need for him.

"Yes," I moaned. Unable to control the need from coming through my voice. "Please, I want it."

He slapped my rear without warning and I cried out. Every nerve in my body was on edge, waiting, anticipating his touch. This wasn't the touch that I had wanted, but it was still something. The blow seemed to reverberate through my bones.

"Call me Master."

"Sorry, Master." I closed my eyes and bit my lip.

How could I be so stupid and forget? It was one of his only rules.

I felt his hands on my ankles and he pulled me towards the edge of the bed, folded my legs under me so my rear was pushed up into the air, my bound arms resting on my back. I grunted, shifting a little as if I could control anything about my position.

He pushed my knees apart until I was utterly exposed and open to him. I pressed my face into the bed, nearly overwhelmed with the exhilarating agony of anticipating for so long.

I felt like I had been waiting for Ezra's cock for hours, no, days. Since he'd first mentioned training on the deck of the Kelpie.

"Please," I said again. I felt his hand on my rear, gentle this time. His thumb rubbing a circle where he'd slapped me. I felt him move closer, some skin pressing against mine, but nothing more than that yet.

I had to do better. I was the pet, I was the one who'd messed up.

"Please, Master, I know I'm not worthy," I mumbled, into the bed. I was thankful now for my position, that he couldn't see my face, that I couldn't look him in the eyes as I said such things. I meant them, but it was also humiliating. "I'm sorry for forgetting but please, please can I feel you?"

I heard him make a low hum that I thought was approval. Spurred on, I continued to talk. To beg. To debase myself for him, because although it was mortifying, I was enjoying it, too. I couldn't deny that. I felt my cock dripping onto the bed.

"Please, Master, I'm yours, yours to use. I want-" *no, wait, that wasn't the right way to ask. Try again.* "Please, Sir, please let me feel your cock? Be so kind?"

"Very well," he murmured, and a wave of relief and pleasure rippled through me. "Since you asked so prettily."

He pressed his cock against me, and I strained back, trying to encourage more. He tsked his tongue against his teeth and gripped my hip with his other hand. "Stay still, pet. I know you want it, but I get to decide how fast you get it."

I moaned, equal parts desire and frustration. But I understood now. It wasn't for me to demand things. It wasn't my part to say how this would go. I was his to enjoy. And he would enjoy me however he saw fit. I breathed out slowly, trying to relax and not strain for more.

Slowly - agonisingly slowly - he pushed his cock inside me. I tried my best to stay still, trembling with the effort and grateful for his steadying hand on my hip.

The drag of him as he pushed inside, the way he filled me up, it was intoxicating. I shifted, trying to stretch myself even more so he could fill me still deeper.

My arms strained against the leather and I groaned with all the varied sensations.

"All right, pet?" Ezra asked when he finally had his hips pressed against my rear, buried deep inside me.

"Y-yea, yes," I stammered.

"Good." He didn't move his hips aside from a gentle roll that threatened to drown me in blissful sensations. His hands moved gently up over my sides, caressing me where the leather was and the spots where it wasn't, every touch seeming to ignite another wave of pleasure.

Faintly, in the back of my head, I wondered if it was possible to faint from desire. If it were possible, I was surely on the brink of it.

Ezra's hand stroked up my arms and found my hair. He tugged the black ribbon loose and my hair fell free. He wrapped a hank around his fist and tugged hard enough that I groaned from the new sensation.

"Ready, pet?" He growled, leaning in to sink his teeth into my shoulder.

"Yes," I said, although I had no idea what he was asking. Surely I couldn't be more ready, more prepared for whatever he was about to do? But I wanted it, I wanted everything.

With that he began to thrust. Pulling most of the way out and then slamming back into me. The impact of it was powerful enough to shake the bed. Suddenly, staying on my knees was a harder task than it had been a second ago.

It didn't matter, I pushed back with what strength I could muster and took his pounding, moaning loud enough I had surely alerted the entire inn, if not the whole town, to what we were up to.

It was Heavenly, although perhaps sinful was a better word for it. My entire body was enjoying the feel of Ezra slamming himself into me again and again, and soon my cock was aching for release. Half afraid it would just do it without any intervention, I began to beg again.

"Please, please Sir," I gasped.

"What?" Ezra grunted. He had been remarkably quiet through this, but I could feel the heat of his skin, the way he was caressing my skull and tugging my hair, his other hand gripping my hip tight, his fingernails digging into my flesh.

"Please, I need to come," I gasped. "Please can you touch me?"

"Mm." He shifted, letting his hand slip from my hip to wrap around my waist, closing around my cock with a firm, hot grip. "In a moment. Hold it back if you can."

He might as well have asked me to hold back the tide. As soon he touched my cock I was pulsing with pleasure.

My mind scattered: how could I possibly resist the inevitable? How could I stop my body doing what it was yearning for, and had yearned for so long?

I squeezed down on him as I reached completion, felt my cock pumping out fluid for far longer than I could remember it doing before. Ezra groaned deep in his throat, thrust one more time into me and filled me himself.

His hand pumped my cock once more and his hips came to a stop.

We both remained in position, me because there was no way to move. Ezra's hand in my hair became a gentle stroke, and we both panted out our pleasure for a few blessed moments of relief.

He pulled out of me finally, tugged on my ankles and I stretched my legs out, wincing a little for they'd been compressed in a kneeling position I wasn't used to.

I heard a jingle and the padlocks on my cuffs were undone, Ezra removed the straps from my arms and I moaned with relief as my arms fell forwards. I stretched them up over my head just to feel the movement in my muscles.

Ezra stroked his hand over my back and then undid the buckles on the harness. Once it was loose and falling off, he gently turned me over, rolling me off of it and setting it aside.

I was still panting, all the thoughts in my head largely gone. Replaced with the remaining pleasure and the sensations of my body.

Ezra moved around, setting the leather paraphernalia aside and pouring me a cup of fresh water from a pitcher on the washstand. I sat up on my elbows and took it from him, drinking gratefully.

"Well," Ezra said, as I licked my lips and took another drink. "What do you think? You didn't say stop at any point."

I drank again, trying to find the words to respond to him. My body trembled once. I handed him the cup back and lay back down.

"Didn't want you to stop."

Ezra smiled, an indulgent smile. "So you liked it?"

"I liked it. Very much." I swallowed, reached a hand out to touch his leg. "I like being yours."

"Good. Just one more thing..." Ezra shifted closer and undid the collar from around my neck. To do this he leaned in, put his arms around me. I pressed my lips to his and kissed him softly.

He kissed me back and smiled a little, maybe I'd surprised him going by the twist of his smile and the expression in his eyes. "You're very sweet."

"Did I do all right? I know I made a number of mistakes, but..." I trailed off as he let go of me, turning to put the collar with the other things. I swallowed wondering if I'd stepped too far with my question, or what was supposed to happen next, but I trusted Ezra would let me know, and besides, I was feeling in need of reassurance.

"It was your first time, properly. You did well, Gideon."

I felt a warm glow in my chest, contentment settling into me.

Ezra picked up a cloth and cleaned us both up with gentle hands. I'd never experienced Ezra being so kind and well, soft. It was very welcome, even a relief, given what we'd just done together. He tossed the cloth aside and settled in against the pillows on his back.

"Come here, pet," he said. I didn't need to be told twice - I settled in beside him, resting my head on his chest, looking up at him. I put my hand on his stomach and rubbed lightly on his skin.

He wrapped his arms around me and kissed the top of my head.

"This is different," I said, smiling. "For you, I mean."

"It's part of the whole uh, deal," Ezra said. "Violence and intensity, it can make you a bit unsettled, even upset. It's important to be gentle afterwards, so that you don't get any of that. It's my responsibility as your master to make sure you're cared for."

I sighed happily. My body was still trembling slightly, but pressing myself against Ezra's warm body, with his arms around me and him saying he wanted to take care of me, was certainly helping to ease the disquiet inside me.

My thoughts were slowly regathering themselves and I realised the intensity of what had just happened. How I had loved the feeling of belonging to Ezra, how I felt, being passive and taking whatever Ezra had given. Trusting that he would deliver me pleasure, and he had.

"So, how do you feel?" Ezra said, his voice quiet and a little rough.

"I feel..." I pressed closer against him, considering. "Wonderful. Like all my bones have gone out of my body and I'm utterly relaxed."

Ezra smiled and leaned down to kiss me. "Good, you really did very well. I'm pleased with you. Proud of you."

The contentment and ease settled even further over me.

"So, is it always like that?"

"Well," Ezra said. "No. I could have tied your legs to the bed. I could have gagged you or put a leash on your collar. I could have punished you and whipped your arse and back until you were a whimpering, quivering mess."

I shivered, looking at the glint in his eye as he described these things.

"I... probably shouldn't find the prospect of that quite so enticing, should I?" I breathed.

"Well, I do, so I won't judge you if you do. In fact, I'd be happy to give you any experience you like, Gid."

I nuzzled my face in against his neck until he laughed,

slipped my arms around his neck and kissed his skin. Of course, I wanted to try all of those things, but for the moment I was quite spent, physically.

"I love you," I murmured into the hollow below his ear.

Ezra squeezed me against him and didn't reply. I suppose I hadn't exactly expected him to reply, but my heart sank a little as the silence stretched out.

I continued to nuzzle him and then relaxed again. I was sure eventually, Ezra would be able to express himself back to me. It would just take time, and I was happy to spend that time with him.

Ezra started to stroke my back and hair, lulling me to sleep.

In the meantime, while I wait for him to say it, we can have more experiences like this one. I know he cares for me. He'll get there, I'm sure of it.

CHAPTER EIGHT - IN WHICH ORA AND GIDEON GO SHOPPING

*I*n the morning I woke up feeling cold, Looking around, I realised I was alone in the bed.

Strange that Ezra hadn't woken me up when he left. Perhaps I'd simply been so exhausted that he'd tried to tell me where he was going but I had continued to sleep?

I had the feeling I'd dreamed something, but I couldn't remember any details of it.

Sitting up, I pulled the blankets around myself. The sun had risen outside, judging from the light coming through the curtains.

What were my options? I could stay in bed and wait for Ezra, but there was no telling how long it would take him to return. I could clean myself and get dressed, go next door to see what Tate and Ora were doing, or I could go off on my own into Tortuga, which seemed like a terrible idea. The worst possible idea. So, not that one then.

I got up and picked up the pitcher of water and a clean cloth and cleaned myself, I hummed to fill the silence in the room a little. The water was cold, and the room wasn't warm so I hurried to dry myself off and pull my clothes on. The leather things Ezra had bought yesterday were all bundled back into the sugar sack so I assumed he didn't expect to come back and do any more training.

I swallowed the lump in my throat and combed my hands through my hair, pocketed my black ribbon and shrugged my coat on over my shoulders. I glanced back at the room and let myself out of room six. I took a few steps down the deserted hallway and knocked on the door to room seven.

There was movement inside the room and Tate opened the door, a dagger in his hand, raised and ready to stab. He visibly relaxed when he saw me, dropping the dagger hand to his side.

"Gideon, good morning. Ora and I were just about to go out and find something to eat."

I instantly felt more at ease seeing Tate and behind him, Ora. They both looked well rested and happy to see me.

Suddenly, I had a lump in my throat and I threw myself into Tate's arms. He caught me, barely rocking back with the impact of me colliding with him. I hid my face in his half open shirt as tears leaked out of my eyes.

"Hey, are you alright? What happened?" Tate's voice rumbled through his chest and I gripped his waist, feeling the solid mass of him grounding me. His arms wrapped around me and centred me further.

I heard Ora move across the floor towards us.

"Gideon? Did Ezra do something? Did he hurt you? I'll skin him -"

"No!" I pulled back to look Tate in the eyes and then glanced at Ora who was looking at me wide eyed, concern written all over their face. "No, he didn't hurt me. Nothing like that."

I swallowed, suddenly mortified that I'd acted in such a way.

Ezra and I had enjoyed a fantastic, illuminating and exhilarating evening together, and here I was acting like a crying baby. A toddler who'd had his toy taken from him.

I shook my head and forced a laugh. "I think, he just wasn't there this morning and I felt lonely. I'm so used to waking up with you. It's silly really, nothing to worry about." I wiped my eyes on my sleeve, pushed myself up onto the tips of my toes and kissed Tate's lips.

Tate kissed back, squeezing me against him. Then I turned and reached for Ora, and gave them a morning kiss too. Tate left one arm around my waist and I felt the warmth of him slowly heating me up.

Ora smiled and kissed me back, then rubbed their cheek against mine, which was more comfort again. How did Ora know so much about what I needed?

"Good morning," Ora said. "Tate and I slept in the bed together."

"You did? How'd you like it?" I asked. I wondered if I should feel jealous of them, but I didn't at all. Tate and Ora were so dear to me, the knowledge they'd spent time with each other filled me with joy. I wanted them to love each other the way I loved them.

"It's was good," Ora said. They looked at Tate and then smiled at me. "We kissed a little, and touched each other but not much. We didn't mate."

I giggled a little. Impulsively, I gave Ora another kiss. "You're adorable."

"So, uh, breakfast?" Tate asked.

"I want to look at clothes," Ora said, after they'd finished eating the bread and cheese the tavern served for breakfast. I was picking at mine slowly, knowing that by all rights I should be hungry, but not feeling it.

"You should buy some clothes," Tate grunted. He was drinking a large ale. "You can't keep stealing from Sagorika."

I snorted. "Isn't it a pirate ship? Shouldn't we all be stealing?"

Tate gave me an indulgent smile. "Not from each other, Gid. You have so much to learn about the pirate way of life."

"I suppose I do," I said, sighing. Ora stole the cheese off my plate and winked at me.

"You have lots to learn about merfolk, too," they said. "All sorts of things."

"But first you're learning about humans and clothing," I said. I pushed my plate towards them and nodded. Ora helped themselves to the shredded bread, happily.

Tate squeezed my arm. "I'll give you some coin to spend."

"You're not going to come with us?" I blinked at him. There was movement across the room that caught my eye, some people were looking at us. I swallowed and pulled my arm away from Tate.

"No, I have some business to do, will only take me a couple of hours and then I'll be back here." He frowned as I pulled my arm back. Tate dug into his pocket and pulled out a handful of gold and silver coins, then a few more and pushed them towards me. "Be safe, you two."

"Of course," I said. "I'll have my sword and Ora has…" I didn't want to finish my sentence.

Tate and I both looked at Ora, who sucked the last piece of bread into their mouth with a slurp and them beamed at both of us.

"Yes. Just be careful, all the same. All sorts of people around this place, and you look like..." Now it was Tate's turn to not want to finish his sentence. "An easy mark."

I sat up straighter, prickled and swept the coins into my pocket. "I don't know what I have to do to prove to you that I can take care of myself," I huffed. "But I assure you, *Captain*, that I can."

"Now, I didn't mean it like that," Tate said. He reached for my hand and I exhaled, annoyed, but I let him take it. I was aggravated, but I didn't want to push Tate away entirely. "I just worry about you because, you know, you dress a certain way. And you're -"

"It's fine," I said. "I'll get myself some clothes, too. Thank you for the money."

I stood up and waited for Ora to stand too. "Gideon, I've been here before, I know what it's like out there..." Tate said but I shook my head.

"We'll see you later."

Ora looked confused, but followed me out of the tavern anyway.

"What just happened?" Ora asked, once we were outside.

"Nothing, everything's fine," I said.

Ora grabbed hold of my hand and tugged me back to look them in the eyes. "You can't lie to me, Gideon, I can smell it. It's radiating off you."

"What is?" I asked, feeling uncertain. "You can smell what?"

Ora tilted their head to the side and tapped their mouth with their finger. "Hurt, sadness which is masked by the anger, fear... You're a confusion, a maelstrom of emotions."

"I'm not sad, or afraid," I said, although I was well aware that it was untrue. I shifted my weight between my feet.

"You are." Ora slipped their arms around me and hugged me

against them. I tried to pull away but Ora held on tighter. "What's bothering you, love?"

Simply their use of that nickname was enough to cut through my irritation enough that I could hug them back.

"It's fine," I said, sighing. "I just want to, I'm sick of everyone saying I can't look after myself, that I look weak."

"Have people been saying you look weak?"

"Well, they've been implying it," I said. I shook my head and pulled out of Ora's arms. There were so many people around, even early in the morning. I hated the idea of people staring at Ora and me together.

Ora's mouth twisted in a way I hadn't seen before, and I felt wretched. I couldn't let my own emotions conflict with a morning shopping with Ora. I'd always loved shopping for clothes, and Ora had never been shopping at all.

I looked out towards the marina, caught sight of the Grey Kelpie and inhaled deeply. The smell of the ocean and the sight of my new home settled - what had Ora called it? - the maelstrom inside me.

It wasn't even as if I disagreed with Tate. I knew it was a terrible idea to go wandering through Tortuga on my own. I knew I was a mark, more than the others. But I didn't like it being pointed out like that.

I took a deep breath and gave Ora a smile.

"Come on, let's find you some clothes."

"I want one of those," Ora said. They pointed at a woman walking past in a long green dress.

"Right," I said. "Let's find the store where they sell dresses."

It was a vastly different shopping experience than the day

before. Ora wanted to see everything, so the walk through the town proper was slow.

"What's that for?" Ora asked, pointing at a dog.

"Uh, it's a pet. Like Zeb was," I said. I flushed because that word had a different meaning to me now, and I wasn't sure if Zeb would like to be called a pet now that he was a human. Or maybe he would? "Before he changed, I mean."

"Mm, and these are for your feet, aren't they?" Ora took my hand and pulled me towards a cobbler's. Their window was full of pairs of shoes and boots of all kinds.

"Yes, you've seen me wear those," I said. "Like I am currently."

"I want to try some," Ora said. They led the way inside.

I sat beside Ora on the stools they had set out for trying shoes on. The store itself was more genteel than I would have expected for a place like Tortuga, and I noticed they had iron bars on the windows. It was run by a lady in a modest but fashionable gown who introduced herself as Delphine.

"Ora's never had a pair of shoes before, Miss Delphine," I said, before Ora said anything entirely strange. "They'd like to try some different sorts on, if you please."

"Of course, dears," Delphine brushed her hands off on her skirt. "Right, you'd better tell me what you like the look of then."

Ora pointed at some pink satin heeled shoes with rosettes on the front. I cringed - they were so unfashionable, that colour! - but didn't say anything. If Ora wanted them, then I'd happily buy them.

Delphine carefully took the shoes down and brought them over to Ora and crouched to help them slip them on.

Ora held their leg out, examining the way their foot looked

with the shoe on. The heel made Ora's calf taut in a very fetching way.

They shook their head. "No, not these ones. What about those?"

Delphine retrieved the plain oyster grey leather slippers Ora was pointing at.

"Those seem a little more practical," Delphine said, tactfully. I nodded in agreement.

"They feel nicer. Much nicer," Ora said.

"Try walking in them, perhaps?" Delphine said.

Ora placed their hand on my shoulder and braced on me as they stood unsteadily. They took a couple of steps, still holding onto me, so I stood too, took Ora's elbow.

"You don't have to walk any differently than with bare feet," I said, softly.

"It feels very different, like I might fall down," Ora said. "They're... oh, I see."

Ora moved a little more naturally but there was still something coltish about the way they held their legs. As if their knees would give out.

"Maybe a pair of boots, next?" I said to Delphine. She nodded and went to peruse the selection.

Ora sat down and gingerly removed their feet from the slippers. "I don't know about any of these," they whispered to me, in a sort of conspiratorial way.

"We'll just get you one pair, in case we ever go anywhere properly civilised. Whichever ones you like the most."

Ora frowned at the room in general. "They look pretty, I thought they'd feel good."

"I suppose we're all used to wearing them," I said, slowly. I couldn't imagine growing up and never wearing shoes. It must feel proper peculiar.

"How about these ones, dear?" Delphine held a pair of short black leather boots.

"Those look good," I said, trying to get Ora enthusiastic about them. "Sturdy, good in a storm."

Delphine helped them into the boots and Ora huffed their breath out and shook their head. "I don't like the feeling around my ankles. If I have to wear anything, then the slippers."

"Lovely, shall I wrap them for you or would you like to wear them out of the store?" Delphine asked, as she unlaced the boots and removed them from Ora's feet. They stretched their toes and sighed.

"Wear them," Ora said. "I have to get used to them if I'm going to pass as a human."

I froze, looking at Delphine's face. It went quite blank, and she continued to remove the boots but she didn't say anything and her mouth slowly became a thin line.

"What a silly thing to say, Ora," I said, attempting to make a joke out of it. "Of course, we're all humans, here."

I had thought this would have made light of it, and eased the tension in the room. Instead it just made it painfully clear that Ora was not human, and seemed to imply that I wasn't either.

"I'm not a hum-" Ora started but I spoke louder, cutting them off.

"Please, just, take the payment." I pulled a gold coin out of my pocket and handed it to Delphine. "And we'll leave immediately. Ora, put the slippers on."

"Yes, thank you." She took the coin and hurried behind the counter. I hauled Ora to their feet and we went to the door. "Wait, your change," she said, but I shook my head.

"Please keep it, I'm terribly sorry to have bothered you. I hope you have a simply lovely day!"

I tugged Ora out of the store and closed the door behind us, we started walking down the street a little faster than we'd been strolling before. Ora tripped a little in their shoes.

Ora looked at me wide-eyed. "Did I say something wrong?"

"Passing for human doesn't include announcing to people that you need to pass for human," I hissed.

"Ohhhh." Ora smiled. "Sorry. Did I embarrass you?"

"No, you didn't embarrass me, I love you. But you might have scared that woman."

"I thought it was all right, there are witches and other things in Tortuga aren't there?"

"I haven't seen anyone like you," I said.

"I can go back and apologise," Ora said, half turning but I shook my head and tugged them back beside me.

"No, it's best we just leave her be now. We'll find you a dress, but first you have to remember to not say anything out of the ordinary."

We turned down a side road that looked to have some clothing shops in it. I looked in the windows.

"But I don't know what ordinary is," Ora said. "How am I supposed to know what's ordinary?"

"Just, try to avoid referring to humans as humans," I said. There were a couple of people coming the other way so I tugged Ora to the side of the path so we weren't in the way.

"What should I say instead? You are humans."

"People, we call each other people," I said. The two men approaching had moved to the same side of the path as us, so I tried to manoeuvre Ora back into the middle of the path.

"Stop pushing me," Ora said. "What are you doing?"

The two men moved in front of us again. They seemed to intend to be directly in our way. I looked into their faces and swallowed. They didn't look friendly.

In fact, they looked exactly like the kinds of men I had expected to find in Tortuga - huge, brutish, scarred and looking at me as if I were something to devour. And not in a good way. One of them had a full beard and worn looking sailor's garb and the other was wearing a black coat with gold fastenings over a dirty linen shirt.

"What've we got here, then?" one of them rumbled.

"Two little fairies with too much money weighin' them down, I'd wager," the other replied.

"I am *not* a fairy!" Ora exclaimed, hotly. I glanced at them and saw their eyes narrowed, their jaw working. I remembered the events on the slaver's ship and put my arm across their chest. My heart started to race. This could go very badly...

"Ora, don't do anything," I said, quickly. I couldn't draw my sword and hold Ora back at the same time.

The men laughed and the bearded one pulled his sword, bringing it to point at my chest. "Best give us all your money."

Ora twitched behind my arm, took hold of me by my waist and pulled me backwards, away from the sword. I stumbled a little, trying to keep eye contact with the ruffians.

"Not so fast," another voice said. My blood chilled. There were more of them. Of course there were more of them.

I chanced a glance over my shoulder and saw a man with a pinched looking face, shorter than the other two, but wiry. He had a dagger in each hand. They didn't even look clean, they were rusted and jagged... the thought of one of them slicing my skin would haunt my nightmares for days, no doubt.

"Hand over the coin and no one gets hurt," Black Coat said. I swallowed.

We were surrounded, and I didn't want Ora to go tearing anyone's throat out.

Perhaps I should just hand over the money?

"All right," I said. I raised one of my hands palm up and stuck the other in my pocket. "You can take it, we don't want any trouble."

Ora started to hum, and I recognised the siren song he'd used back at the Splintered Isles to subdue Solomon.

"Ora, no!" I said urgently. "There's too many people around. Too many innocents." Ora went quiet again, I could feel the tension in their grip on my waist. They were trembling, and I imagined it was less from fear than it was from holding themselves back.

"Hurry it up." Beard raised his sword to under my chin and I inhaled, closing my eyes, pulling the coins out of my pocket.

Please Mother, if you're watching, please let this go well.

There was a thump, and the sword was gone from my throat. I opened my eyes to see Zeb standing in between Ora and me and the two who had initially accosted us.

The man's sword was in Zeb's hand, and he was aiming it at Beard's throat.

"Zeb?" I exclaimed.

"You leave Gideon alone," Zeb said, a bit too loud and a bit too much like a yowl. "You don't know who you're dealing with."

"What's your game?" Black Coat growled. He pulled out a flintlock pistol and aimed it at Zeb.

Zeb didn't hesitate, he ran Beard through with his own sword and, immediately after, leapt on Black Coat, punching him in the face.

Ora turned behind me and grappled with the pinched face man. I drew my sword but I hardly needed to. Zeb dragged his sharp nails down Black Coat's face and moving almost too fast to track, was hauling Pinch Face off Ora and slamming him against the wall.

In barely twenty seconds, all three would-be robbers were on the ground, wounded.

Beard's sword stuck out of his chest and he groaned, blood bubbling from his mouth. I let my sword arm drop down again.

"Are you all right?" Zeb asked, crossing the distance to me in two strides and taking me by the shoulders. He peered into my face, his eyes wide.

"I, yes, I'm all right. Ora?"

Ora's face appeared next to Zeb. Their hair was tousled but they appeared unhurt. My heart was pounding but the relief washed through me like alcohol. "I'm all right."

"Perhaps we ought to get back to the inn," I said, faintly. My ears had started to buzz, and I saw spots.

It's just the shock of it, keep breathing, a voice in the back of my head said. I sucked in a ragged breath.

Ora slipped their arm around my waist and Zeb took my sword off me.

We made our way back to the Pickled Oyster in silence. I was unhurt, but the knowledge of what could have happened had shaken me to my core.

Fairies, they called us fairies.

They knew we were lovers and that was one of the reasons they wished to attack...

What would they have done if I'd been alone?

CHAPTER NINE - IN WHICH THERE IS ONLY ONE HUMAN IN THE ROOM

*B*ack at the inn, Ora led the way to room seven. We stood and looked at the door for a moment.

"Do you have the key?" I asked.

"No, Tate does," Ora said.

I knocked on the door, just in case Tate was back from whatever business he'd had, but there was no reply. I eyed the door to number six but I wasn't sure that seeing Ezra right now was what I needed.

"Stand aside," Zeb said, impatiently. He bent to look at the lock, crooked a finger and inserted a rather long claw into the lock. A few moments later he had the door open.

"How did you do that?" I asked.

"Claws," Zeb said. As if that explained anything at all.

Ora locked the door behind us and I went to sit on the bed.

Zeb followed and sat beside me, pulled me against his side and started to purr.

"I don't understand," I said. "You have claws some of the time and nails the rest of the time. You had a tail and pointed ears during the fight with the slavers, but not now. How can you purr like that? Humans can't usually purr."

"Well, you are the only human in this room," Ora said. They kicked off their slippers and came to perch on the other side of me, sitting cross legged.

"Oh. We didn't get you a dress," I said. "I'm sorry, Ora, we should go out again."

"Not now, though," Ora said. "You're even paler than you usually are. You need tending."

"Afraid," Zeb said softly, still purring. "Needs comfort."

"What were you even doing around there, Zeb?" I asked. I leaned against him as well, he was nice and warm, and I didn't want to talk about my needing comfort or being afraid again. That all felt like it would lead to talking about me being weak and needing protection.

And the sick feeling in my gut that Tate had been right, and maybe I did need protection. I really didn't want to think about that.

"On the roof," Zeb said. He slipped his arm around my waist and pulled me closer still.

"On the roof why?" I pressed against him a little more. I wished I could purr.

"High places, you can see all the things going on. My queens didn't recognise me," he said. "I looked around everywhere."

"I'm sorry," I said.

"S'fine," he said. "Got you, got Ora. Tate, too. Maybe Ezra, later."

Ezra.

I sighed and Ora started plucking at my coat. "Maybe you'd feel better if you laid back?"

"I feel all right," I said.

"Mm, Ora's right." Zeb let go of me and started tugging my coat off my shoulders. Ora tugged it off by the sleeves. Zeb's fingers went to my shirt and started fumbling with the buttons.

Ora shifted closer behind me and kissed the side of my neck. My neck was so sensitive now that as soon as their lips touched me I felt a thrill.

I breathed out, leaning back against Ora and let Zeb pull my shirt off. He stroked his hands over my chest and nuzzled the other side of my neck until I was panting.

I was in the act of reaching for Zeb's hair to pet him when he sat up, raised his arms over his head and lay back against the pillows, loose and sprawling.

"You may worship me," he said, his voice a little more gravelly than before.

Ora moved to the side and we eyed each other. "Worship?" Ora asked.

"Mm, c'mere," he said. He reached a hand out to us and folded the other under his head.

We looked at him, stretched out on the bed, his shirt hanging open and revealing his deep brown skin over his muscular chest, the way his stomach stood out in hard muscles and the hint of pointed black ears pointing out of his thick curled hair.

His eyes were half closed, his legs spread loosely - utterly obscene in those black leather pants that hugged his hips and his thighs. I felt heat spread through me.

I glanced at Ora and saw their mouth quirk into a mischievous smile.

I pushed my worries, my fears and annoyances to the back of my mind. Perhaps I'd feel better if I lost myself in these two not-quite-human lovers of mine?

"I... think I know what he means," I said. I stood up to get rid of the rest of my clothes. I was uncertain if I'd have any marks on me from the night before, but now wasn't the time to check. I climbed up on the bed beside Zeb. I gently stroked my hand up his chest and teased at his nipple with two fingers.

Ora took very little time pulling their skirt and blouse off and moved to settled on the bed on Zeb's other side. They rested their head on Zeb's shoulder and reached to undo the lacings on his leather pants.

"That's right," Zeb said. He moved an arm down and put it around me, settling his hand on my rear. I inhaled, moved closer into him. I leaned my head down and kissed his collarbone and up to his neck. I felt him purr through my lips. Smiling at how simple a thing that purr was, and how appealing in this form, I kissed a slow trail up to his lips.

He kissed me back aggressively, pushing his tongue against my lips until I opened them. I hummed as his tongue explored my mouth. The kiss was rough and unpractised to be sure, but it had a fire, a passion to it that was stimulating.

I broke the kiss to catch my breath and Zeb moaned, arching his back. I looked down to see Ora with their mouth closed around Zeb's heavy cock and moaned myself. Ora's full lips were juicy looking and they bobbed their head, giving Zeb and me an arousing show that left me breathless.

Zeb's hand carded through my hair and he tugged me in for another kiss that stole what breath I had left, for a moment. I rocked against him, grinding my cock against his hip, needy.

"Up here," he said. "Get on my face, Gideon."

His blunt language probably shouldn't have been shocking to me, by this point I wouldn't have thought much would be, but I still felt myself blushing all the same.

Ora moaned and pulled up from their position. "Yes, you ride his face, and I'll ride his cock," Ora said. Both of them were so direct, so uncivil. There was really no point in being fussy about it, and besides, the suggestion was utterly appealing so why would I fight it?

I shifted with some difficulty, until Zeb grasped me by my hips and positioned me with one knee on either side of his shoulders and my rear over his face, facing Ora. He leaned up to lick at my hole and I gasped out loud, almost lost my balance, only Ora was there. They straddled Zeb's hips and reached out to brace me with their arms. I gripped them gratefully.

Ora sank down on Zeb's cock with a groan that I couldn't help but echo as Zeb's tongue explored me intimately.

It wasn't a rough session of fucking and ownership the way it had been with Ezra the night before. This was slow, gentle by necessity as Ora and I balanced over Zeb. I shifted my hands to Ora's shoulders and leaned in to kiss them, groaning at the salty taste of Zeb's arousal on their tongue.

Ora began moving their hips like the exotic dancer I'd seen when we first arrived in Tortuga. I remained as still as possible, letting Zeb do much of the work.

Although, he did say to worship him... I wouldn't want to disappoint. I'm not officially Zeb's pet, but I'd wager he'd like it if I focused on giving him pleasure.

I let go of Ora with one hand and trailed it over Zeb's torso, teasing at his nipples again and scratching at his skin.

His hands were still on my hips and I gasped as he probed into me in such a deep and intimate way I felt I might come apart even without my cock being touched.

Ora was squirming, their body undulating, one hand gripping my shoulder, the other braced on Zeb's stomach as they rocked faster and faster. I trailed my hand down Zeb's body and closed it around Ora's cock, stroking them as they gasped.

Zeb's body bucked suddenly, his hips thrusting, his hands on my hips yanked me up and tilted me forwards, into Ora's arms, and his mouth closed around my hard and dripping cock.

Without warning I came, the stimulation from Zeb's mouth and the suddenly close up sight of Ora bouncing with the thick cock inside them too much for me.

Ora and Zeb seemed to come together in the same moment. Zeb bucked off the bed and Ora fell backwards with a happy sigh.

I rolled off Zeb's face and we lay in a tangle of limbs, sweaty and panting.

And that's how Tate found us when he opened the door with the room key.

CHAPTER TEN - IN WHICH THERE IS REVELLING

"*W*hat on Earth have I got here?" Tate asked, laughing as he walked into the room. "I thought you were going clothes shopping."

Tate's walking in startled me, I must have been drowsing, and I half sat up. "We tried, but there was a complication." I licked my lips. "Someone tried to rob me, well. To rob us, and Zeb intervened."

"After that Gideon was afraid so we came back here."

Tate's face turned thunderous. "Who was it? I'll track them down and keelhaul them under the Kelpie."

"No, it's- it's fine," I said. "I wasn't *that* afraid." I shook my head and reached a hand out to Tate, wanting to placate him. "They didn't actually take anything."

The last thing I need is Tate picking a fight with some thieves for my honour.

Tate sat on the edge of the bed and took my hand in both of his, pressing it between his large, warm hands.

"To think I could've lost you, and over what? Some old debts?" Tate shook his head.

"Is… it that what you were doing? Paying off old debts?" Ora frowned, leaned over my legs and looked Tate up and down. "But you still have all your limbs. Did they take teeth?"

"Stars, Ora." Tate's eyebrows drew together and he shook his head. "No, they took money. What kind of place did you come from again?"

"Under the sea," Ora said with the tone of explaining something to a dull child. "Debts are paid from the body."

For a moment, Tate and I gazed at Ora while they looked back at us, eyes wide.

Then Tate shook it off and I cleared my throat and I took Ora's hand with my free one and pulled them towards me.

"I'm glad you're safe up here with us," I said. "Well, thieves and pickpockets aside."

"You weren't in any real danger," Zeb rumbled, still partially underneath me. I tried to shift off him, but his hand closed around my thigh and held me in place. "I was watching."

"Yes, Zeb dropped from above."

"Was on the rooftops," Zeb said. "Easier to get around up there, less people."

He sounded half asleep, and I glanced at his face. His eyes were closed and his chest rose and fell with a steady rhythm.

"My life," Tate said, amused. "I mean, it was already plenty interesting, but since you waltzed into it, Gid, my life has become so much more interesting. He tugged me into a kiss that I returned with warmth.

"Come on, whoever wants dinner, put some clothes on and I'll treat you downstairs." He let go of my hand and stood up. "Food and drink."

Ora slipped off the bed and picked up their skirt and my

shoulders sagged as I remembered the failed mission of our shopping trip. "Ora still needs a dress," I said.

"I'll take you tomorrow morning," Tate said. "No one will bother you when you're with me."

"I don't mind," Ora said. "I'm still not sure about shoes."

I shifted, going to get off the bed but Zeb dug his fingers into my thigh. "Zeb! I'm getting up." I tried to twist away from his grip but then I felt his fingernails dig in.

"Stay and sleep," Zeb grunted.

"I want food," I mumbled.

Thinking back to when we used to have battles over the best spot in the bed when he was still a cat, I had an idea. I reached my hand into his hair behind his ear and scratched him gently. Zeb's face split into a contented smile and he relaxed his grip on my leg.

"That's it," I murmured, trying my best to soothe him as I kept scratching. "That's a good kitty."

"Not a kitty..." Zeb sighed, and his head dropped to the side, his hand fell away from my leg and he was snoring gently.

I eased myself off the bed and smiled down at him, pleased with myself.

Tate chuckled behind me then caught me up in an embrace. Laughing I turned in his arms and kissed him, feeling nothing but happiness.

"Very impressive," Tate said. "Who knew that would still work on him?"

"We should bring him some fish," I said. I felt my heart swell with fondness for Zeb, the kitty-turned-man and for Tate, my gorgeous Captain, for Ora who was eyeing up their leather slippers as if they were about to do battle, and for Ezra, although that was still tinged with a little hurt. I hadn't talked to him since last night, and I wasn't sure at all what I wanted to say.

Tate squeezed me against him and let me go. "Put some clothes on, Gid."

I caught my breath - he had near squeezed it out of me - and nodded, getting dressed as quickly as I could.

The sun was setting as we claimed one of the Pickled Oyster's tables near the large windows.

"I like looking at all the people out there," Ora said. "There's so many people."

"Yes, you should see London some time," I said. "Probably a hundred times as many people there."

"Sounds smelly."

I dusted the chair off with a handkerchief before I sat, as there seemed to be some old crumbs of bread or something on it.

"Yes, I suppose it is, a bit. But the buildings are very impressive."

Tate had placed an order at the bar as we found the table and joined us after a moment, crashing into a seat and beaming at the both of us.

I smiled back, finding myself rather looking forward to an evening of food and drink with Tate. But I had to ask...

"Have you uh, have you seen Ezra at all?"

Tate shook his head. "But I'm sure he'll be along soon, don't you fret."

"I wasn't *fretting*," I said. But I felt my cheeks warm because it was a bit of a lie. I had been worrying about seeing him again, poking at the tender feeling like it was a scab I couldn't leave alone. Not that I thought of Ezra as a scab. But the lost feeling I'd felt this morning hadn't really gone away, and I didn't like to think of it, but I was all the same.

"Dinner, lads." A beautiful woman with flowing brown curls, golden brown skin and large dark eyes set a tray on the table. It was laden with two jugs of ale, three large plates of roasted meat and vegetables and an entire loaf of fresh baked bread. My stomach rumbled noisily but thankfully it wasn't heard over the general noise of the pub.

"Thanks, Lyssa, you're a honey," Tate said. She smiled and rolled her eyes.

"Yes, you got extra butter, I know, I'm an old softie," she said. "Sing out if you need anything else, all right?"

"We will." He smiled and winked at her and she grinned and went back behind the bar.

We ate and drank together. It was hard not to relax in the Pickled Oyster. I was getting accustomed to the people around us being pirates, prostitutes and various sorts of vagrants. What had shocked me the day before now seemed familiar.

Surprising how quickly one can adjust to previously shocking things...

The tables were polished wood and the chairs were unexpectedly comfortable. I relaxed against the back of mine, content to stay quiet and watch Tate and Ora.

Someone in the corner of the pub started to play on a violin - a jaunty sort of tune, which added a merry atmosphere to the place. Although everyone around us was drinking and veritably bristling with weapons, no one seemed to be fighting or making trouble.

Tate downed his beer in record time and poured another from the jug.

"Go on, drink up, both of you," Tate said. He pushed our tankards closer to us. Gamely, I lifted mine and took a deep draught of it although the taste was bitter compared to the wine I was used to drinking.

Ora took a sip and then set the tankard down, grimacing. "Tastes rotten," Ora said.

Tate laughed a hearty belly laugh and clapped Ora on the shoulder.

"Room for one more?" I looked up and my heart thumped hard in my chest. Ezra.

He wasn't looking back at me, but focusing on Tate. Tate nodded and kicked a chair out from the table for him.

"Aye, and take Ora's beer, they decided they don't have the taste for it," Tate said. Ezra caught the chair and sat, nodded at me and picked up the beer, drinking from it.

"Evening, everyone had a good day?" He asked. His voice - that familiar growling hoarseness - struck me deep in my stomach, and I was pleased to see him and upset at the same time.

I mirrored his actions and drank from my beer, hoping the alcohol would burn off some of my confused and conflicting feelings.

"I took care of some business, Gid and Ora here almost got robbed," Tate said. He picked up a roast chicken leg and started eating it messily.

Ezra half turned to look at me. "You did?"

"Mm, Zeb intervened," I said lightly. I drank some more beer, it was tastier the further down the tankard I got. Tate refilled it for me from the jug.

Ezra's hand fisted on the table and he scowled. "Who was it?"

"It's taken care of," I said quickly. I was sure Ezra had been about to declare he'd find them and do something unspeakably violent to them the same way Tate had.

"Did they hurt you?" Ezra's hand moved onto my knee and squeezed it gently. "They'd better not have or there'll be some serious trouble tonight."

"I'm fine," I said, stiffly. I drank some more beer and didn't manage to look him in the eyes.

"Mm," he said.

Ora yawned wide and stretched their arms up over their head. "I might go for a swim, sleep out in the harbour tonight," they said.

"You had enough to eat?" I asked, reaching to squeeze their hand.

"I'm good." Ora nodded and stood up, leaned in and gave me a warm kiss. "I'll see you in the morning, Gideon."

"Love you," I said without thinking. I looked around but no one in the place seemed to have even noticed that we'd kissed, let alone what I'd said afterwards.

"Love you, too," Ora said. They gave Tate a kiss on the cheek and wiggled their fingers at Ezra before making their way to the door.

"Stay safe," I called after them, feeling slightly bereft.

"They'll be just fine, Gid, nothing to worry about," Tate said. He topped my tankard up again. He turned to Ezra. "So what, exactly, were *you* doing all day?"

"I had some correspondence to take care of," Ezra said. His tone made it clear he wouldn't elaborate or explain. I was itching to know who Ezra could possibly be writing to, and the ale gave me the courage to pry.

"Who do you correspond with?" I asked, leaning forward on one elbow. My head felt quite light by this point, I propped it on my hand to stabilise it.

"Just... family," Ezra said. He looked away, down at the table, instead of meeting my eyes. I looked at Tate who shrugged one shoulder - the meaning was clear enough *if he doesn't want to talk about it, then I'm not going to ask.*

"Your parents?" I ventured. "Do they know what your, uh, profession is?"

"My family is aware I voyage and send home money," Ezra said. "I saw something at the postal office - some bills posted, looking for one Gideon Keene and requesting his safe return to Kingston."

My blood went cold and although I knew Ezra was simply changing the subject to avoid answering my question, the thought of people looking for me here, on this island I had thought was safe, was chilling.

"What's the reward posted?" Tate asked, and I remembered his suggesting my return, the bounty collected and then coming to steal me in the night. I felt a thrill of excitement at the intrigue of it, but quickly dismissed that.

"Hundred pounds," Ezra said. He eyed me and then Tate and shrugged. "Doubt we have anything to worry about here, most keep to their own and the bounty isn't high enough to be too worrying. But I thought you'd like to know all the same."

"Hmm," Tate said.

"Is a hundred pounds a lot?" I asked, I mean, in terms of Naval wages it was a substantial amount, more than a whole year's work, but I had no idea what it meant in terms of a bounty.

"It's not nothing," Tate said. He frowned at Ezra. "How much was yours up to last you saw a bill?"

Ezra shrugged. "Five hundred, or maybe it was up from that. Didn't look for myself on there."

"What did you do that was so bad?" I leaned towards Ezra, then regretted it as my head spun. "I mean, I know Father wanted to hang you, but *why*?"

Ezra looked at me and laughed. "You're drunk, pet."

"You're avoiding the question." I stabbed my finger at his chest and prodded him with it. "What did you do?"

"I embarrassed him," Ezra said. "That's all."

I shook my head. I knew my father, and he wouldn't be so angry over a little embarrassment. Even if Ezra was referring to his honour being besmirched, I suspected it had to have been more than that as well.

Maybe I could convince Ezra another way, he had called me pet after all.

I moved my chair closer to Ezra's and leaned in, ducking under his arm and pressing my palm to his chest, acting coquettishly as a heroine from one of my beloved romance novels.

"Ezra, you can tell me..." I leaned in and kissed softly at his jaw.

Ezra groaned, part amused and part aggravated. I heard Tate cackle across the table. Emboldened, I moved closer, put myself half in his lap. "Please?"

"I used to have my own ship," he said. "And I looted and sunk your father's merchantman. A big one. Lots of money and goods."

My eyes widened a little. I thought I could remember the day he'd had that news, maybe? My memory was foggy, it had been many years ago, perhaps when I was nine or ten, but he had been in such a temper. He'd stormed around the house... thrashed the servants, anyone who came close. Probably would have thrashed me except that I knew well enough to hide in my room and bar the door.

I shivered and Ezra closed his arm around me, his hand curling on my waist. I leaned against him.

"Was that all, though, why would he have such a vendetta for you after all this time?"

"Well, he did catch me once," Ezra said. "But that's a story for another time."

I opened my mouth to ask another question but Ezra crashed his mouth against it and then we were kissing and all thoughts flew out of my head. He undid me with his lips and then deposited me back in my chair.

I suppose two can play the seduction game to get what they want, I thought, a little mulishly.

Tate saw my expression. "Aw, Gid, it's not that bad." He turned in his chair and called towards the bar. "Lyssa! More ale!"

The rest of the night passed in something of a blur, as the ale quickly overtook my logical mind. I recall at one point, Tate dancing to a tune played on the violin, spinning the barmaid Lyssa in and out of his arms.

I recall taking her place next, and allowing Tate to spin me just as vigorously across the floor.

I recall laughing over something utterly mundane with Ezra and Tate.

I recall stumbling up the stairs to Tate's room, where Ezra joined us in a happy tangle on the bed - waking Zeb, who woke up the instant he smelled the fish I had managed to procure.

I recall messy, delicious sex with three men and falling asleep rather abruptly directly after.

CHAPTER ELEVEN - IN WHICH NEWS IS RECEIVED

*W*hen I woke up it was because of two things. No, it was three things. The first was that my bladder was near exploding and the pressure to relieve myself had become painful. The second was that Ezra had moved, and that had made Tate move, and Zeb had grumbled loudly, and flopped directly on top of me, and put more pressure on my bladder.

The third thing was the loud knock on the inn door.

"Zeb," I groaned, and shoved at his shoulder. He wasn't as large as Tate but it was a close enough thing that my shove had absolutely no effect.

Tate sat up. "Who's knocking?" He bellowed.

The noise split my skull and I groaned again. I tried to squirm out from under Zeb but he seemed to be getting heavier somehow. I ran a hand through his hair, hoping that would wake him. I noticed some grey hairs threaded through his black ones.

He's an old cat, I suppose.

"It's me," Ora called. "The door's locked!"

Tate got out of bed, and apparently Zeb had been partially

leaning on him too because Zeb slid off me enough then that I could escape. I went to make use of the chamber pot. I leaned heavily with one had against the wall.

I felt utterly terrible. My mouth was dry, my head pounded and relieving myself didn't entirely alleviate the ache in my gut.

"Mornin' Ora," Tate said, opening the door to let the merfolk in.

Ezra sat up, shoving Zeb off him.

It makes sense that he only stayed in bed over night because he was drunk. And Zeb was allowed to cuddle him.

"You're warm," Zeb whined and pawed at him, trying to pull him back in.

"Not interested in cuddling right now," Ezra growled. "Or ever, really."

I hadn't quite been able to move away from the chamber pot so I watched this exchange with interest. Both Zeb and Ezra were somewhat dominant and seeing the two of them together I had to wonder what it would be like if the three of us were to have sex...

My stomach turned over and I closed my eyes, willing the nausea away.

Chamomile tea and plenty of it, that'll see you right in no time, Gideon, my darling. My mother's voice in my head, how she had carefully looked after me when I was sick.

I doubt you'd want to coddle me when this illness is entirely of my own making, and I woke up entangled in three naked men...

Ora was saying something in an urgent tone, so I forced my eyes open, pushed away from the wall and went to listen.

"Some leagues away at the moment, but getting closer," Ora said. "The dolphins said it was definitely Navy."

"Fuck, damn and blast," Tate said. "I wanted to lay low here longer, a week if we could manage it." He went to pick up his clothes and pulled them on without hesitation.

"What's happening?" Ezra grumbled, his face half squashed in a pillow.

"You can talk to dolphins?" I asked.

"We have to set sail," Tate said. "Naval ships nearby."

"Set sail? But..." I wanted to protest this but I didn't really have any reason to. What was I going to say?

Ora wants a dress? I wanted to explore Tortuga more. Maybe take Tate to the leatherworkers and see if he'd wear that thick black collar for me?

These are all preposterous notions.

I cast around, looking for my clothes and pulled them on. Ezra had scrambled up and was going the same. Zeb turned over, one eye open and watched us all moving.

"Come on, Zeb," Ora said, moving to his side. They stroked a hand down his head and spine and Zeb let out a brief purr. "You too."

Zeb grumbled, stretched and sat up, yawning hugely. "What about breakfast?"

"Whatever you can find that won't take time," Tate said. "Come on! We have to hurry."

He was buckling on his sword, his eyes flashing. I hurried to pull on my boots. Ezra - already fully dressed - went next door to collect his things from his room.

Soon enough we were boarding the Kelpie. Once we were outside in the bright sunlight, Zeb had offered to run around Tortuga and round up any crew who were on shore. Ezra ran a small blue flag up the second mast to indicate the crew should return.

Tate watched the shore as we waited, tapping his foot and sighing with every passing minute.

Within an hour, the Kelpie was taking advantage of morning winds and tide to sail out.

Getting back onto the ship in such a hurry was unpleasant - I had been looking forward to breakfast at the Pickled Oyster. But at the same time, I couldn't deny that being back on the familiar polished wood deck was comforting. This boat had become home to me, and knowing that soon we'd be just us again - the crew and nobody to see us - relaxed the tension I hadn't realised I'd been holding in my shoulders.

Zeb, having rounded up all the last members of the crew, climbed the rigging and settled in a crow's nest. I shuddered to watch him climb it, my old fear of heights extended to watching others who I cared about dare to climb.

Ora went to the bow of the ship, stripped off their clothing and slipped overboard once the ship was out of Tortuga Harbour. My heart thumped a little with concern over them as well, although I knew better than anyone that Ora could take care of themself. The little bits of information I learned about merkind were alarming though, and I hoped they wouldn't encounter anyone unfriendly.

Ezra deposited his sugar sack of purchases from the leatherworkers below deck and took the helm. Tate was pacing the ship.

First going to his cabin to examine a map, then heading to the prow of the ship to study the horizon with his spyglass. Then he'd return to his cabin, swearing.

I intercepted him after what felt like the dozenth repetition of this pattern.

"Tate, Captain." I put myself directly in his path and he stopped short, his face stormy.

"What is it, Gid?" His tone was short, irritated.

"What's the matter?" I said. I pulled myself up to my full height, which was still a good foot shorter than Tate and folded my arms.

"If it's not urgent then you can get out of the way," Tate growled.

I had to force myself not to cringe back, although my heart was racing, the pulse of it pounding in my throat. He was so tall, and so angry - it could have been my father storming around, and my instinct was definitely to hide - but I knew Tate.

I knew how kind and caring he was, and how unlike him it was to act in this manner. I was confident that if I could get him to talk about it, then he could calm down.

"It is urgent, you're storming up and down the ship. That doesn't exactly seem like important work to me. What's the matter with you?"

Tate folded his arms, mirroring my posture and smacked his lips. "Nothing's the matter with me."

"All right then," I said. "Then you won't have any trouble if I suggest we go to your cabin right now and relax in bed."

"I can't do that," Tate practically spat the words.

"And why not?" I arched an eyebrow. I felt a little like I'd become one of the preparatory school teachers who liked to give out detention. However it seemed to be working, so I continued to look as severe as possible.

Tate's mouth twitched and he dropped his arms. "All right, I'm pissed off. I wanted to have some more time in Tortuga. I hate feeling like I'm running away. I want to stay and fight but I know that in this case it would be suicide. So we're running, but I hate it."

I smiled and unfolded my arms as well. "There, now, that makes sense. You're allowed to be angry about that, but like you said, it's a sensible course of action."

Tate nodded, dragged one hand through his hair and looked away, sighing.

"Is there anything else bothering you?"

He looked back at me and narrowed his eyes. "Maybe. Maybe I was afraid of losing you. When you told me about the thieves, I just…"

Warmth flooded my chest and I went up on my toes to kiss his cheek. "Tate."

He wrapped his arms around me and hugged me tight to his chest, one hand pressing into the small of my back.

"You mean so much to me," he whispered with a fierceness that I recognised, mirrored in the power of my own feelings for him.

I put my arms around his neck and kissed him firmly on the mouth. "You mean so much to me. I love you, Tate. So, so much."

He pressed his forehead to mine and for a moment we just stayed like that in the middle of the deck. Holding each other and wrapped in a fierce love that felt all consuming for just a moment.

He let go of me and licked his lips. "Your father is serious about getting you back. That means we need to be serious about making a plan to keep you safe. Maybe we need to distract him, or throw the scent off somehow."

"Surely we can just stay ahead of them," I said.

Tate grunted and shook his head. "It's the best plan we have right now, it just rubs me the wrong way."

"Maybe you can find someone to rub you the right way?" As soon as I realised I'd said something so salacious I felt my cheeks burn. "Oh God, what just happened?" I mumbled.

Tate laughed heartily, took me by the waist and kissed my cheek. "You're ridiculous. And you're unusually confident right now, for you. I'm into it. It's exceptionally alluring."

"Yes, I don't exactly know what's got into me." I rested my cheek against his chest.

"Almost reminded me of my old commanding officer," he said. I pulled back from his chest, surely I hadn't heard that correctly? I looked up at him.

"What commanding officer?"

"From the British Navy," he said, as if it was nothing. "Didn't you know?"

"No, I didn't know, you haven't talked much about what your life used to be like." I stepped back and looked him up and down. No, he still looked exactly like the pirate hero of one of my romance novels, every inch of him dangerous and unspeakably attractive. I squinted, tried to picture him in a naval uniform but I simply couldn't see it.

"Well, I was. Five years, working my way up," he said.

"What happened?"

"Well, a couple of things. I wasn't good at taking orders, so I missed a few shifts of watch, let my duties on board slide. I couldn't see the point of hopping to it just because someone with a white wig told me to. Then they caught me stealing from the bursar's lock box."

"Ah," I said.

"And I didn't stick around for a court marshal or a

dishonourable discharge or whatever they would have done. I'd met Solomon by then, so the two of us took the rest of the money and sailed away on a stolen ship."

He grinned, showing me all his teeth. I wondered if I should ask more about Solomon, but decided against it, after all we had more or less run away from that problem as well and I didn't want to remind Tate. He seemed happier now, less angry, so I hugged him again.

"I would have liked to have seen you in a Naval uniform though," I muttered against his chest.

He laughed and patted my back. "Maybe I can steal one someday, show you what it looked like."

I pulled back to look at him and scrunched my nose up. "No, I want you as far away from the British Navy as it's possible to be. You and Ezra and the rest of the crew."

"That's the plan." He leaned down and kissed the end of my nose, making me laugh, and let go of me. "In the meantime, thank you, Gideon, I feel better now."

My heart flushed with happiness, knowing that I'd intervened at the right time and given Tate something that he needed. It was a good feeling. He walked back to the helm at a more relaxed pace and I moved to the side of the ship, looking down at the waves and allowing the happy feeling to sit in my chest a while longer.

I hadn't really had friends back in Kingston, let alone lovers, and knowing that something I could do or say would make someone close to me more at ease? It was a new and welcome feeling. Perhaps if I had siblings, or a Father who didn't seem to hate everything that I was, I would have known about this already.

But I was learning now, I supposed, and that was better than nothing.

As I watched the sunlight glittering on the waves, the foam from the Grey Kelpie slicing through the water, a sadness slowly overtook the cheer I had been feeling.

My stomach shifted unpleasantly, as I realised it had been thoughts of my father that had caused this change of emotion. I missed him, despite myself. I missed my mother too. I hadn't spoken to her properly in a while. I felt guilty.

Maybe I should go to my old cabin and chat with her portrait for a bit, reconnect with her?

My eye caught movement in the waves and Ora's face broke the surface. In full mer-form, Ora's skin was grey and had a shiny, scale-like quality. Their hair was damp, curls clinging to their forehead and when they smiled I saw their terrifying sharp teeth.

"Hello, Gideon!" Ora said. "Are you all right? You've been staring at the water for a while now. Do you want to swim? Jump in, I'll catch you." They lifted their arms out of the water, and I saw webbing between their fingers.

"No, I'm fine," I said. I shook my head. "Thank you, but I'd rather stay on the ship for the moment."

Ora flipped their tail, pushing themself sideways as the ship moved. I marvelled at the power of their body in this form - how easily they could keep up with the two masted galleon.

"Well, I'll come up then," Ora said. They turned and dived underwater. I hurried to the bow where Ora's sleep netting was strung under the bowsprit and watched as their lithe, naked form emerged from the water and hauled themself back up onto deck.

I held out Ora's clothing for them and they sighed and dressed themself. The fabric clung instantly to their damp form.

Ora slung a dripping arm around my shoulders and kissed my cheek, their lips cool from the ocean. I shivered a little, mostly from the soggy arm around me but turned my head and kissed them on the mouth.

"I'm sorry we couldn't get you a dress," I said. Ora shrugged.

"It's fine, Sagorika said I can have one of her old ones."

"Still," I said. "It'd be nicer for you to have your own, one that you'd chosen for yourself. I'd have enjoyed watching you turn on a few different ones."

"Tortuga was fun, though, wasn't it?"

"Mostly," I said, smiling at some of my memories. My stomach still felt vaguely queasy from the night before. Ora and I sat down, leaning our backs against the side of the ship and looking back at the rest of the crew. I felt a little guilty that I wasn't helping with sailing in some way, but Tate hadn't requested I do anything.

"I liked seeing so many people," Ora stretched their legs out in front of them and wiggled their toes. "I didn't know humans came in so many different types."

"You didn't?" I chuckled a little. "How many people had you seen before you met me?"

"Just sailors and Solomon really," Ora shrugged. "My people, they don't really..." they paused and I glanced at them to see their head tilted to the side and their jaw working.

The queasiness in my belly flared up, but this time more because of fear than ale. Ora hadn't spoken much about the merfolk but most of their revelations had been highly unpleasant.

"Don't really what?"

"They don't care if I travel, if I leave the clan for a time and explore the oceans, but involving myself in the human world is frowned upon."

I leaned my shoulder against theirs. "I'm sorry."

"Don't be sorry," Ora lifted my arm and cuddled under it, pushing more against me. "I love you, and I want to stay with you. But before you, it was just drowned or near-drowned people and Solomon, and Solomon isn't like other humans."

"That's true enough," I said, shuddering. I still felt our business with Solomon was unfinished, and that was another worry to add to my pile, along with... "Your family, uh, your clan I mean, would they hurt you? If they knew what you were doing?"

"Yes, I think so," Ora said. They sighed and hummed a little trill and the queasiness in my stomach subsided a little. "But it's all right, they don't know and they don't have to know. They'll think I'm exploring the ocean, which I am anyway."

I turned my head and kissed their temple. "What is it like down there?"

"We don't have towns like Tortuga," Ora said. "We have clans and warlords, territories, but there's lots of unclaimed ocean as well." They shrugged. "I don't know how to talk about it, really."

"That's quite all right," I said. Although a part of me was disappointed and did wish to learn more about merfolk, I didn't want to make Ora uncomfortable or remind them of unpleasantness. I wouldn't insist on anything.

Instead I pulled them closer against me and wrapped my other arm around them and pressed myself to them. Ora slipped their arm around my waist and for a moment we just held each other.

Ora's hand squeezed my waist and then dropped down to

caress my hip and I sighed happily, feeling the stirrings of arousal.

Ora pulled back to look me in the eyes with a curious expression, their lips pouting and their dark and perfectly arched eyebrows drawing together.

"What is it?" I asked. My heart thumped uncomfortably. Ora had seen or sensed something unusual and they were looking at me, but I couldn't be the cause of it, surely?

"There's something about you," Ora murmured. My heart leapt into my throat.

"There-there is?" I asked, my voice somewhat strangled.

Ora titled their head and gazed into my eyes with an intensity that made me want to look away, to hide, but what was I hiding? Ora knew me, from the moment we'd met it felt as if our souls had aligned somehow. I would never hide anything from Ora intentionally. My skin prickled and then Ora shook their head and shrugged.

"I don't know, there's something... almost magic about you. But I don't know what it is."

"Magic? Me?" My nervousness made me laugh but I could hear how uncomfortable I sounded.

"Maybe?" Ora shrugged again. "I don't really know, I just sense something. We'd probably need a witch to tell for sure."

I frowned, thinking of my time with Solomon. He'd been able to use magic on me easily, surely if I had my own magic I'd have felt his, or... been able to repel it?

"If Solomon was able to spell me truthful, and put me to sleep seemingly without effort, doesn't that mean I'm not magic?" I asked, taking Ora's hand and threading our fingers together.

Ora shook their head. "No, Solomon is very powerful, and

whatever it is inside you, there's not a lot of it. Or... or maybe it's sleeping."

But... I had resisted him a little, hadn't I? I recalled words tickling at my throat and biting my tongue to resist speaking them out loud. *What had he said to me then?*

"Solomon said there was a strength to me," I said, slowly, recalling the way he'd said it. "But that I might not know about it yet."

"There's lots of strength to you," Ora said. They squeezed my hand and smiled. "But I think maybe he was seeing something more as well. Maybe this. Maybe there's more to you."

"Wait, what did you mean when you said it was sleeping?" I shivered involuntarily.

"I don't know, maybe like a kraken sleeps at the bottom of the ocean, and then one day it will rise up and..." Ora cleared their throat. "Eat a lot of people is what krakens do, but in your case maybe it just means one day you'll wake up and your magic will be at the surface. It's only a guess though."

I frowned, I didn't like the idea of something sleeping within me, kraken-like, ready to surface and eat people, or maybe consume me from within.

"What does it mean? Perhaps, maybe I could be a witch?"

Ora shrugged again and sighed. "I don't know. We'd have to find a proper witch to know for sure. We can't answer that now, so don't worry about it."

I sighed, leaned back against the side of the ship and looked up at the sky and the sails. Easy enough for Ora to say that I shouldn't worry about it, but the fact was the conversation had set an unpleasant swirling in my stomach and I had to swallow a lump in my throat.

"Oh, I made it all worse," Ora said. They leaned their head on my shoulder and slipped an arm around me, squeezing.

"It's fine," I said. I didn't want Ora to be concerned over me, so I sat up a little straighter. "I'm quite all right."

I shoved the unpleasant feeling in my stomach down, swallowed hard and cleared my throat, forcing my own swirling emotions to the back to focus on Ora instead.

I kissed them lightly on the mouth and smiled again.

"Gideon," Ora said, their voice soft and flooded with meaning.

They are about to bring up feelings again, and I can't handle it, I think... if we talk about the implications of what it means that I could somehow have magic, I might cry, or fall apart. I can't do that. I have Zeb, Ora, Tate, and Ezra to look after. I have to be strong for them.

"It's all right," I said, kissing them a little more firmly. "I should talk to Ezra, soon. Clear the air there, perhaps." I swallowed, because the idea of doing that was repulsive as well, but again, I had to be strong.

I stood up, Ora's hand falling from my waist and walked down the deck. I would talk to Ezra, and I'd go to my cabin and visit with the portrait of my mother. But perhaps, I'd do those things in the morning.

The sun was going down, and we had started the day in such a rushed panic. There had been hours of idleness and soon there'd be dinner. I could put off the hard work of talking to Ezra until the next day.

That night, Tate, Zeb and I went to bed together but we all fell asleep rather than get up to anything salacious.

Tomorrow... I thought, more of a promise to myself, or my cock, than anything else. *Tomorrow we'll have some fun with these men.*

CHAPTER TWELVE - IN WHICH EZRA ADMITS SOMETHING

I woke when Tate got up in the morning, and I lazily watched him get dressed and clean his face.

Zeb got up shortly after and I managed to doze for a while longer. Finally I got out of bed, washed myself and pulled on a soft white shirt and short brown trousers.

I wish we had been able to go clothes shopping and not just for Ora, I thought sadly. *I am getting heartily sick of these plain clothes from home.*

I sought out some breakfast from the galley and went up onto deck, eating the bread and cheese I found there. I glanced up at the heights of the main mast and saw a long black tail hanging down from the crow's nest. I couldn't suppress a shudder.

"How can he stand to stay up there?" I murmured to myself. My heart thumped dully with fear, the idea of being up there compounded with the terrible thought of Zeb falling down and hurting or killing himself. He hadn't been human for a long time, but I had a real affection for him. Perhaps because I'd had such affection for him as a cat and he still acted largely the same.

Aside from the talking of course, and the fascinating things he could do with a human body.

I shook my head and looked around for Ezra, quelling the stirring in my groin as I thought of Zeb's firm chest and the... rest of him.

Ezra stood a little back from the helm and Tate had his hands on the wheel. They seemed to be talking about something serious.

"Too much cover," Tate said, shaking his head.

"Cover can work to hide us as well as it hides our enemies," Ezra said.

Ezra noticed me and did a sort of head nod greeting so I approached. Things on the ship were sort of unclear in terms of hierarchy and who should know what - I hadn't been sure if I should interrupt the First Mate and the Captain speaking. Even if they were my lovers.

"Hello," I said.

"Good morning, Gideon," Tate said, smiling easily. I eyed Ezra who gave me a brief smile. "Did you want something?"

"Oh, uh, yes, I suppose I wanted to talk to Ezra," I said, stiffly. My discomfort at the thought of talking about emotions with Ezra was making me go all preparatory school formal again. I shook my head at myself. "If you're not too busy, I mean."

"Not busy," Tate said. "Take him away."

Ezra rolled his eyes at Tate and folded his arms. "What's that supposed to mean?"

"It means go off and do whatever it is you need to do," Tate said. He chuckled. "What on Earth else would it mean?"

"Come on, pet," Ezra said. He unfolded his arms and stalked away. I widened my eyes at Tate who shrugged and smiled.

"Enjoy," Tate said.

My stomach clenched again but I turned to hurry after Ezra, who was headed below deck. He led me to the spot by the brig where we had first had sex together, just the two of us, and the memory of that made my skin flush warm in the dim light.

I mustn't be distracted.

"What is it, pet?" Ezra asked. He turned and it seemed as if his expression softened some. I looked into his eyes and willed myself to say what had been bothering me.

"The other night," I said and paused to swallow. My mouth felt so dry. "The night in Tortuga, after we went to the leather works..."

"You want more, do you?" Ezra moved closer to me and I had to tilt my head to look up at him. I breathed out heavily, my cock hardening at the proximity of his body and the promise in his voice. The memory of the leather straps tightening around my torso and my arms. It was all too delicious and yes, of course, I wanted more.

But that's not what I wanted to say. But maybe I should just forget it, he's clearly still interested in me. If there was a reason he was gone in the morning, it wasn't that he doesn't like me, or want me. He just had business, and I'm blowing it all out of proportion.

"Yes," I said. I forced the next word out of my throat. "But."

His eyes narrowed a little. He hadn't touched me yet. Unlike my other lovers, Ezra didn't often touch or kiss me casually. His power was in what he didn't do, and what he stopped me from doing, and the incredible pleasure that came from the withholding.

"But?" He prompted. His arms folded over his chest again. "Well, spit it out."

"I..." I took another heavy breath. I hated that this was so hard, that so much of me seemed to be resisting expressing myself. But what about when he had cuddled me after, and said that was all a part of it? I was allowed to ask for what I wanted, wasn't I? "I hated that you weren't there in the morning, the next day I mean," I said, finally.

Ezra's eyes widened. "Oh?"

"Yes, I woke up, and you were gone and there was no note or... well, I suppose I wouldn't have expected you to leave a note, silly of me to say that, but I... I felt uh, rather, bereft." I said.

"Bereft?" Ezra echoed back and I felt distinctly that he was now laughing at me.

That stirred something else in me. Annoyance.

"Yes," I said. I pulled my shoulders back and straightened my spine and met his eyes. "Bereft, because what we shared, it was incredible. I loved it. I loved being yours, and I loved falling asleep with you. But when I woke up alone in that bed, it felt like you'd abandoned me."

Ezra took a half step back and his amused expression vanished, replaced with something blanker, more defensive.

"I didn't-" He started but I wasn't done.

"I felt as if, as if..." I searched my soul for the true meaning of how I had felt, why I had been sad. "As if you had used me like a whore, and that - that I meant nothing more to you than one. I felt dirty, and ashamed, but mostly I felt sad. The depth of that sadness..." I shook my head. "It hurt, Ezra."

"I didn't mean to hurt you," he said, quietly.

"Well, you did," I said. I felt bolder now, perhaps I had been expecting he'd laugh in my face or tell me I was overreacting but he wasn't, and that meant perhaps my feelings were valid. The tone of his voice and his expression bolstered me up. "And I don't know what I needed exactly, except that I wanted you to be there with me."

Ezra took a deep breath and nodded finally. Then he did something that I hadn't expected, he took me in his arms and pulled me close against his chest.

"I'm sorry, Gideon," he said, into my hair, his voice gruff.

I hesitated for a moment before I put my arms around him, but it was purely because of how unexpected his reaction had been. With relief, I wrapped my arms around his waist and pressed my face against his shoulder.

I felt the anger trickle away, replaced with a wave of love and affection and attraction that soon had me pressing against him tighter, my hands fisting in the fabric of his shirt.

Ezra shifted and then pulled back to look me in the eyes and I blinked up at him, my breath coming quicker now.

"Really," he said. "I'm sorry, pet. It's just that, well, I've never felt anything for anyone like I do for you..." he paused, seeming to search for words. I held my breath. "I don't know what it is, but you invade my thoughts, and I find myself thinking up more and more complicated ways to make you mine."

I swallowed, my curiosity piqued, but I didn't want to interrupt his explanation so I stayed quiet and let him fill the silence in his own time.

"I don't think I could share you with anyone, if you were... if we didn't..." He shook his head and I could see the struggle in his eyes. His jaw worked as he looked for the words. I held my breath. "If I couldn't see how much love you have to give. I know I could never give you everything you need. I'm not... I'm not at your level of accomplishment for love and affection. So I'm happy that you have Tate and Zeb and Ora, because I don't feel a lack of attention from you, you don't feel any less mine when it's just the two of us." He sighed heavily and shook his head, gave me a lopsided smile. "Is any of this making sense to you?"

I let my breath out and kissed his mouth. "Yes, that makes sense, and I'm so glad. Because I love being yours, but I love being with the others as well."

He squeezed me against him and kissed me harder, this time it was more of what I thought of as a signature Ezra kiss, a sort of battle that he wanted to win. And perhaps more importantly, I wanted to let him win. I pulled him close to me again and he spun us, pressing my back against the wall and kissing and kissing me.

When he pulled back to look at me, a question in his eyes, I was utterly breathless, clawing at his shoulders and back and trying to pull him back in. My blood seemed to heat me all over, and then pool in my stomach and down to my crotch.

He didn't move, and I realised he was waiting for a verbal response.

"Please," I gasped. His eyes went hooded and he kissed me harder still, his teeth closing on the flesh of my lower lip and tugging hard enough to hurt.

I tore his shirt open and stroked my hands over his skin, there was an urgency throbbing through me that I couldn't deny, didn't want to deny.

"Want to bend you over and fuck you so hard you can't remember your own name," he growled. His voice seeming to penetrate every fibre of my being and set it aflame.

"Oh, good Lord," I breathed.

His hands moved to the waistband of my trousers and I moaned, rolling my hips into his hand so he could touch me there. His hand slid inside and stroked me and it took a lot of my willpower not to come on the spot.

But I can't, he'll want me to hold it back for his command, and I want to please him and obey.

Then there was a sound that caused Ezra to freeze entirely.

The ship's bell.

The alarm.

CHAPTER THIRTEEN - IN WHICH
THERE IS A TERRIBLE BATTLE

*E*zra swore and pulled his hand off me, and although I knew he had to attend to the alarm, I whimpered. He gave me a swift kiss.

"Come on," he said. "We'd best see what the problem is."

I swallowed hard and fastened my trousers with trembling hands. I'd never been interrupted like that before.

Ezra moved fast and I had to hurry to follow him up the stairs and to the deck. We saw the problem immediately. The small islets and islands we had been passing had somehow concealed a British Naval ship, which the Kelpie had sailed towards. They had moved close to flank our ship and they didn't look like they wanted a calm conversation.

"This is going to be rough!" Tate shouted. He'd left the helm in the hands of Shem. "Ready the cannons!"

Ezra hurried to Tate's side so I followed him, my heart pounding with fear now, arousal utterly forgotten.

"Gideon, you get into my cabin and stay low," Tate said.

"No!" I shook my head. "I can help, I want to help."

"I gave you an order," Tate said, looking at me sharply.

My blood ran cold. I set my jaw, despite the fear coursing through me - how could Tate talk to me like that?

"Tate, I want to help, I know how to arm and fire cannons, I was drilled, I know what to do!"

"This is not negotiable," Tate said. I looked into his face and saw something hard in his expression. I was reminded of the initial fear and awe I felt when I first met Tate - this gigantic, powerfully muscled man who could tear me apart with his bare hands if he really wanted to. I swallowed.

"Orders, Captain?" Ezra said. He looked between the both of us, his expression giving away nothing.

That's right, in times of battle Tate is the true Captain, and his word is law. I shouldn't have argued with him.

"Take Gideon to my cabin and lock him in if necessary," Tate said. My breath caught in my throat and my back stiffened in indignant anger. But Tate's the Captain. It's not my place to contradict him.

"Yes, Captain." Ezra's hand closed over my bicep and he towed me towards the door to Tate's cabin. I had enough dignity left not to kick or scream or resist - although some spoiled, childish part of me wanted to. I had enough of my wits about me not to distract the crew from the imminent attack.

Zeb dropped down from the rigging and looked curiously at the both of us.

"Orders from Tate," Ezra barked at him. Zeb raised his eyebrows and sauntered towards the cannons. The deck was a mass of activity. The crew were unlashing cannons, rolling out barrels of gunpowder, lighting brands and shouting to each other. Tate's voice booming over the top with more orders.

"Ezra, please," I managed to say, as we approached the cabin. "I need to prove myself."

"Captain's orders," Ezra said again. "And besides, you won't distract me or the Captain this way. Stay down, be safe. Don't worry."

"Distract you?" I asked, indignant, my voice going shrill.

He shoved me inside and the door slammed. I stumbled, tripping over my own feet and landed with a crash on the floor.

Perfect. Whatever dignity I had is gone now. All of the crew would know I was kept out of the way, locked in a room like a damsel who can't defend herself.

I pulled myself up into a sitting position and gazed at the door. I had no doubt Ezra would have locked it behind him. I slowly got to my feet and tried the handle just in case, but as I expected, it was locked.

After the last battle nobody has any faith in my fighting skills - they don't think I can protect myself.

The very fact that Ezra had said I could be a distraction to him or Tate made me feel even worse.

Based on the evidence, they didn't just think I couldn't protect myself, but that something about my being out there would turn their heads.

They'd be so busy looking at me - probably trying to protect me - that they'd make themselves vulnerable. Like a British Naval Officer would stab Tate while his head was turning, trying to find me in the melee.

There was a roaring boom from out on the deck and the ship shuddered. I stumbled back to the bed and sat down.

The battle had started. And there was nothing I could do now, because the door was locked and I was thrown in the cabin to be kept safe.

Ora and Zeb would be fighting. I chewed my lip. I knew both of them could handle themselves in close quarters. I'd seen them. I'd seen Ora tearing out throats and Zeb with his claws and his fearlessness.

But this wouldn't be hand to hand combat... hopefully at all. From the glimpse I'd got of the Naval ship, it was far enough away that hopefully the Kelpie could sink it with a few well aimed cannons.

I don't want to wish that many men dead, I thought, sadly. *But I definitely don't want the Kelpie to be boarded.*

Ora and Zeb had no experience with ship to ship battles and although I was sure that Tate and Ezra did, every battle was dangerous. Experience was a great asset, but so much of this was down to chance.

The very fact that the Navy were firing on us meant we could sink, and then most likely no one would survive.

Trapped in the cabin I had nothing to do but listen, and wring the bedclothes between my hands and let my mind go in circles about what might be happening outside.

What if someone was injured? What if the ship took too much damage? What if they do board us and overwhelm the crew? Tate and Ezra would be headed for the gallows and I back to my father.

I could hear feet running up and down the deck outside. I could hear Tate shouting orders, although I couldn't make out the exact words until he roared "FIRE!"

The noise of cannons firing drowned everything out, the blast and roar and the way the ship shook. I could feel a pull as the ship turned.

My old Naval Captain sprung to mind, unbidden. *"The angle of the ships is everything. You need a clear shot at your enemy's side, without providing too much of a target for them. Aim for the mast, or the hull."*

Ships didn't manoeuvre quickly and time was short. We

couldn't let them get too close either. I dropped the blanket from my hand and stuck my fingers in my mouth, chewing on the nails.

There was a terrible crashing noise and the ship shuddered. I tore the tip of the nail off my left index finger and winced at the sharp sting of it. What had that crash been? Were we taking on water now or was the damage less disastrous? I had no way to tell.

I got up off the bed and paced the room as Tate might have done. I said every swear word I could think of as I did so, but it didn't make me feel any better. My stomach was a knot of tension and it felt as if my shoulders were up around my ears.

I wished for the battle to be over, and for Tate and the Kelpie to have won.

I prayed for the safety of each of my lovers.

I cursed Tate and his decision to lock me in. The frustration of not knowing what was going on was terrible. My stomach ached.

The ship deck shivered under my feet and I lost my footing again and crashed to the ground.

Maybe I should just lie here until it's finished? I thought, dismally.

And for a moment I did. I lay there, pressing my cheek against the cool wood and despairing in my own uselessness.

But I remembered my mother's voice. *Gideon, my sunshine, what are you doing down there?*

I closed my eyes, remembered her picking me up off the path when I'd tripped over - I must've been about six years old. I had fallen down and started wailing, simply despairing over everything and feeling as if there was no point to anything and I may as well stay on the ground.

Mother had lifted me in her arms, kissed my cheeks and bounced me until I laughed again.

I sat up, ashamed of myself for an entirely new reason now. I resolved to pull myself together, and moved back to the bed and sat down again, tucking my legs up under myself to get a little bit more balance.

I still hadn't spoken to my mother's portrait - and now there was a chance I wouldn't be able to ever again. I gazed at the wall of Tate's cabin, the other side of which was my old cabin, Mother's portrait safe inside.

But no, thinking like that wouldn't help anything at all.

There was another din of cannons firing, from our side. I took a deep breath. I wasn't entirely sure that, if God was out there, he'd listen to such as me - who had run away from home to take four lovers at once, undoubtedly a sinner in the eyes of the Church - but just in case, I sent up a humble prayer for the ship.

Please, let us win. Please, Lord.

Let Tate, Ezra, Ora, and Zeb be safe and I'll try to be a better man.

An interminable amount of time passed - shaking decks, loud crashes, the boom and crack of the cannons and shouting, and then finally it died off. I heard cheers from the deck outside the door. I stood up, still tense, and went to the door, waiting for someone to remember about me and open it up.

The noises from outside were certainly laughter, cheers and whoops. That was a very good sign. Something unknotted in my chest.

The deck shifted again and I felt the speed the ship now had. Tate must've ordered we speed away.

I shifted from one foot to the other, infuriated once more

that I'd been locked away and kept from the action. Kept in the dark about what had happened and where we were going now.

Another interminable wait had me pacing the room again, until finally I heard the sound of the key turning in the lock and the door opened. Tate was on the other side.

"All right?" he asked.

I walked determinedly towards him, feeling I must be looking as frightening and thunderous as Tate in a rage.

"How *dare* you!" I exclaimed.

"Now, lad, I know it can't have been fun for you in here -" Tate said. I prodded him in the chest with my finger.

"No, it wasn't *fun* it was absolute *Hell!* I didn't know. I *don't* know, is anyone hurt?" I stepped back and looked him up and down. He seemed to be in one piece. "Are you hurt? Did we lose anyone?"

"No, we're all still alive," Tate said. "Come on out and take a look."

He stepped back and I strode past him with as much dignity as I could manage, tossing my hair. I looked around the deck. There was some damage, a chunk taken out of the main mast, although the sails were intact.

I turned back to Tate. "What happened?"

"See for yourself," Ezra said, moving over from one of the cannons. He pointed behind us and I went to the side of the ship to see - a grand Naval galleon, sinking slowly. The prow of her pointing up to the clear blue sky. There were a number of lifeboats and several men in them and in the water.

My heart thumped dully.

This was the best outcome we could hope for, but still... All those lives. At least we were close to some islands, hopefully many of them would survive. I hated them for attacking us but I also hoped that they would live, and go on to have happy lives, somehow.

Ora came hurrying over, their eyes wide and sparkling with excitement.

"That was amazing!" They said. "I've never been in a ship and ship battle, it was so loud!"

I shook my head a little. I couldn't stand to hear Ora so happy about it when I'd missed out on the battle itself, and now could see people in the ocean. People who might drown.

"What is it?" Ora stopped dead in their tracks. "You're a maelstrom again."

"I'm not," I snapped, and turned away from the sight of the sinking ship. Suddenly the ship felt far too small, I wanted to be alone - and not locked in the Captain's cabin but truly alone in my own space.

I went back to my old cabin, pushing my way past the crew as they secured the cannons and congratulated each other on a job well done.

I felt sick to my stomach, desperate for some peace and quiet to gather my thoughts.

Then Tate appeared before me and I had to stop.

CHAPTER FOURTEEN - IN WHICH
GIDEON EXPERIENCES A MAELSTROM

I couldn't physically get around the Captain. I couldn't look him in the eyes either. Humiliation and anger prevented me.

"Gideon, I know you'll be angry with me," he said. "But please let me explain."

My cabin door was so close, effectively blocked by the sheer mass of Tate.

"I don't suppose I can stop you," I said, as icily as I could manage. I lifted my chin to give him a cold stare as well, although it felt wrong to do so and my heart wasn't in it. Some part of me knew I was blowing this entire situation out of proportion.

Tate folded his arms. "Right, well, it was for your own protection."

"Because you think so little of me that you thought I would be a liability in the battle, yes, I understood that much."

Tate sighed and shook his head, his long brown curls shaking loose over his shoulders. "No, Gideon. We couldn't let the Navy see you," Tate said.

"What? Why? I don't understand."

"If they recognised you, if they'd got word somehow to the rest of the fleet, it could have got back to your father with pigeons or something. Then he'd have known which ship he should be targeting."

I hadn't thought of that. I swallowed a sudden lump in my throat. "Oh," I said.

He took hold of my shoulder with his massive hand and squeezed. I didn't shrug him off, although the temptation flared up in me like a wicked flame.

"The thought of losing you," Tate began. He shook his head once more and I looked into his warm green eyes and felt my heart melt a little. "I couldn't bear it. I had to hide you."

I frowned. "Well, I hated it. You have no idea how awful I felt in there, alone with all of you out here possibly being blasted to pieces. I was utterly useless and afraid."

"I'm sorry," he said, finally. And I sniffed, swallowed a lump in my throat. "Can I hug you?"

And although a large part of my heart wanted nothing more than to let it all go and let Tate hug me until I didn't feel anything but warmth, I wasn't ready to give in to him quite so quickly. "Not yet," I said, finally. "I need a little time."

Tate's hand dropped from my shoulder and the lump jumped into my throat again but I pushed past him and into my cabin, pulling the door closed behind me with a bang.

Once I was in my little cabin again the anger softened into sadness. I didn't like refusing Tate, but I also didn't like how he'd dealt with me.

"Why couldn't he just tell me about staying hidden to start with?" I turned to look at the portrait of my mother and sat on the bed, gazing at her. "Why didn't he just explain it?"

Mother smiled back at me, warm and understanding and full of love - like always.

Oh my darling boy, I imagined her saying. *Think now. What was his priority?*

I sighed and leaned back against the pillows.

He'd had to protect the ship, first and foremost.

Stopping to explain the why to me wouldn't have been a good use of time, I supposed, but also, it wouldn't have taken him that long, surely?

I closed my eyes, trying to will the maelstrom of emotions inside me still. Ora was right, although I had snapped at them - I felt an absolute tempest inside.

My fear, the sadness for the dead, the anger at Tate, feeling useless and pathetic, it was all swirling inside me. Now grief surging inside me for the men in the water, then the conviction that I could never be good enough for my lovers would crash over me instead. And there, in the back of my mind, lurking like an eel in the coral, what Ora had said about my possibly having some kind of strange magic in my blood.

What did that mean, do you know Mother? I opened my eyes to look at her.

You told me stories at night, strange fairy tales of magic and love, but you never said anything about real magic... were you a witch of some kind?

I found that theory hard to believe - she had never behaved as anything but a loving mother, a doting wife. If she had truly had magical powers, surely she'd have displayed them at some point.

Solomon could never pass for ordinary in polite society. The magic in him had corrupted his body - and likely his mind - so whatever it was, Mother hadn't been that powerful or perhaps if you were a good witch it didn't show in your body.

Could it possibly have been Father's side of the family? But I discarded that idea instantly. My father was so relentlessly proper, mundane and, well, closed minded. There was no way he could be secretly hiding magical abilities.

Unless, all of that was an act to hide more effectively? That was possible wasn't it?

I rubbed my hand over my face and groaned. I didn't have enough information to puzzle any of this out. There was simply no way to discover what either of my parents may or may not have hidden from me.

Ora was right, I'd have to ask a proper witch for information, and information such as that would not come cheaply. I think I had some money from Tate still, the treasure we'd looted from the slaver as well. Tate hadn't officially given me a share, but I'm sure there was something there.

A sound at the door startled me. A scratching. Zeb.

I tried to ignore it, uncertain if I wanted company. But just as being ignored had not deterred him in cat form, he continued to scratch.

"Zeb," I called out, tiredly. "You know how to open doors now."

The door opened and Zeb came inside, a huge, gorgeous man with deep brown skin and scars that somehow made him more dashing.

"You're sad," he said, bluntly, and sat on the bed beside me.

"I suppose..." I pushed myself up on my elbows and looked at him, curious. "You can tell?"

"Obviously," Zeb said. He rolled his eyes. "I can always tell when you're sad. I can tell if people are sick too. Always have done."

"Wait, so when you were a cat, too?"

"Yes." Zeb huffed his breath out and climbed half on top of me, leaning a lot of his weight on my chest so I collapsed back onto the bed.

It was actually quite comforting, the warmth and the weight of him. I slipped an arm around his waist. He rested his chin on my chest and looked into my face. Rather confronting, and also incredibly like when he was a cat and I'd tell him all my worries. But with the added complication that I was now desperately attracted to him, and he was pressing on me, and I was getting hard under him.

"So, um," I said, trying to distract myself a little. "Can you change back into a cat?"

Zeb shrugged. "Haven't tried."

"Oh, right," I said. I cleared my throat, his weight was starting to make it difficult to breathe. "Could you try?"

"Probably."

He shifted, put an arm beside my shoulder and dragged his body more on top of mine. Breathless, I swallowed. "What are you doing?"

"Making you feel better," Zeb said. "Cause you're sad." Then he leaned in and kissed me, all tongue and delicious distraction.

My fingers tightened on the back of his shirt and I dug my heel into the bed, pushing my cock up against him to feel that delicious friction.

There was a knock at the door.

I pulled myself back from the kiss and looked over Zeb's shoulder to see the door open and Ezra move into the room.

"Uh, didn't mean to interrupt," he said, gruffly. Zeb didn't move off me, but he dropped his head to kiss at my neck.

"You're not..." I broke off into moans as Zeb sunk his teeth into my neck and my body pulsed with hot need.

"Join," Zeb grunted, licking at the spot he'd bitten and causing me to moan louder still.

"There's no room in here," Ezra said. He moved closer, watching how Zeb was mouthing at my neck. My hips bucked again and Zeb slipped a hand down to my hip, pinning it to the bed and I whimpered, needy and wanton. "But maybe..."

He had something dangling from his hand, I realised, the sugar sack, and I closed my eyes, feeling my arousal grow even hotter.

"Lord, preserve me," I breathed.

Zeb sat up then, slid off me and to the far side of the narrow cot, allowing room for Ezra. The two of them eyed each other up.

"I thought you might want to work off some tension," Ezra said, dropping the bag beside the cot. "Tate told me you were angry, sometimes this can help, give you perspective. Besides, we were interrupted earlier.

I swallowed and pushed up on my elbows again. "I was angry because he made me helpless," I said. "I don't see how giving myself over to your will could solve that."

"Ah," Ezra said. He sat beside me, pushing my hips hard against Zeb's. "You'd be surprised. When you choose it, you have the power, remember?"

I did remember. And Ezra had that sparkling glint in his eyes and the very sight of the sugar sack was apparently all I needed to get another jolt of heat through my body.

I glanced back at Zeb then. He was fond of giving orders too, laying back and telling me what to do... But both of them together? They couldn't *both* be in charge, could they?

"I-I'm, I'm interested, only I feel like we should establish something, I-I," I stuttered. "Who... who's in charge?"

"I am," Zeb said. He went to his knees, leaned over me and kissed Ezra. To begin with, it appeared that Zeb was doing what he'd done to me a moment ago, pulling Ezra apart with the movements of his tongue and the passion in those lips.

But then I saw something shift in the action of the kiss, Ezra growled low in his throat and pushed his jaw forward. I could see both of their mouths moving, and my hand slipped down to stroke myself through my trousers at the sight of the two of them. Apparently, they were battling for domination through kissing.

Ezra's hand moved up to grip the back of Zeb's neck and he pushed forward again. Forcing Zeb back against the wall of the cabin until his back hit it.

The kiss broke suddenly and Zeb ducked his eyes. "Ezra." he murmured. I saw, because I was watching from so close, the two black pointed ears emerge from his hair and smiled at the sight of it. Some magic was terrifying but this was rather endearing. I knew the ears and tail came out when he was angry or defensive, but he'd also had his tail to balance and climb the rigging - perhaps they came out when he was exceptionally relaxed as well, or when he was submissive?

Who could guess what it meant?

"That's right," Ezra said. He reached into the sack and pulled out some pieces of leather. "I didn't plan for two, but I think I can make this work."

"You planned?" I gasped, my hand was still rubbing myself and even through the fabric it was making me breathless.

"You know better than that," Ezra said, slapping my wrist and pulling my hand away from myself. "Sit up, both of you."

I bit back a grumble and did as he asked, pulling my shirt open and tossing it aside as I did so. Ezra slipped my collar around my neck and kissed me roughly, then quickly moved to do the same to Zeb with a thick black collar.

I swallowed against the leather and licked my lips, my skin prickling with desire.

"Clothes off." I quickly removed my trousers and kicked them aside, then turned to help Zeb remove his.

"That's very good. Zeb, hold Gideon's arms back for me."

Zeb took hold of my arms and pulled them behind my back. I groaned, tugging against his hold just to see how tight it was. He held me fast and I bit my lower lip.

Ezra moved to the side and slipped a soft piece of thin leather down my cock, pushing it right to the base and knotting it so it hugged tight and firm around my hardness.

I whined, it made everything that much more urgent feeling. I remembered the first time we'd ever had sex and how he'd held me with his fingers in just such a way.

"Tell me," Ezra said. "What do you think this will do?"

I swallowed, afraid of the answer, but inflamed by it as well. "I-I, I believe it will stop me from completing, Sir," I said. My cheeks flushed.

"Still so formal," Ezra murmured, and smiled, kissing my cheek. "Yes, pet. This will keep you on the edge until I'm ready to release you. Now, let go Zeb."

Zeb let go of me and stroked his hands up my sides instead, making me shiver with pleasure.

"I didn't say you could do that," Ezra said. His tone was sharp but he had a smirk lingering around his mouth. He pulled a set of straps out of the bag and licked his lips. "Gideon, help me with this."

"What is it?" I asked. For a brief, jealous moment I thought he might be using my chest harness on Zeb, but I realised his one was a black leather one, matching the collar Zeb had on.

"Arm binder," Ezra said. "Slip it around his arms, avoid the joints."

I moved behind Zeb and did as I was told, and although I had half expected Zeb to struggle and whine, just to be difficult, he submitted to this quite easily. Perhaps it was because as I worked, Ezra was stroking one of Zeb's furry black ears and kissing him hard again.

Zeb whined into Ezra's throat and I bit my lip - watching them together made me so hard and so hungry for more. The arm binder wasn't complicated, just a series of three straps connected to one that went the length of his arms. I pulled the top strap over his biceps, then the second one went around his forearms. The last closed tightly around his wrists, and the overall effect was absolutely stunning. I stroked my hands over his bound arms with wonder, leaned in and kissed his shoulders where they strained back, and felt a familiar rumble through his skin. Zeb was softly purring.

I looked over his shoulder at Ezra, wondering for one rebellious, inflaming moment what Ezra would look like in straps of black leather, a collar locked around his neck and his muscles straining against the bindings.

I wonder if he ever would consider being the one not in charge? Because I would very much like to see if I could undo him.

It didn't seem like the correct moment to ask about it.

"Good work, pet," Ezra said. He moved his hand from Zeb's

to mine, ruffling his hand through my hair and then softly tugging on it.

I moaned, both from the words and the action. He tugged on Zeb's collar and pulled him forward so his chest met Ezra's knees. Ezra pulled his trousers open and guided Zeb's mouth onto him.

My breath caught in my chest.

"Like the look of that, don't you?" Ezra's hand closed on the back of my neck and pulled me closer, beside Zeb. He let go to pull his shirt off and then guided me to lick at his nipples.

I did this with extreme abandon, pushing my face in to lick and suck at him.

"That's it," he murmured. He grunted, his chest heaving with his quickening breaths, and then pulled the both of us away from him. Zeb sat up, licking his lips. His eyes were half-closed and he looked content.

Ezra stepped out of his trousers and pulled my leather cuffs out and something entirely new from the sugar sack. Something I hadn't even realised he'd been looking at, let alone purchased. It was a riding crop.

He saw my eyes widen and smiled wide, showing all his teeth like a wolf.

"Like the look of this too, do you, pet?"

I swallowed, both fearful and more aroused, and knew he could read all of that in my face. I nodded, not quite trusting my voice if I were to speak.

"Well, I can hardly expect you to stay still for this, can I?" He fastened the cuffs around my wrists and padlocked them in front of me with a final-sounding snap. Now the cuffs were locked to my wrists and to each other, and my breath hitched again.

"How many blows with the crop do you think Gideon needs, Zeb?" Ezra said, idly. He swished the crop through the air with a flick of his wrist and I heard the faint whistle of it through the air. My mouth was dry and I couldn't imagine what this was about to feel like.

"I don't know," Zeb said. "Let's see how red his skin gets from five?"

I groaned softly. "Turn around, pet," Ezra said. "Put your head in Zeb's lap and lick him while I give you your lashes."

I was glad he'd tied my hands in front, then, as it allowed me to lean forward on my forearms and position myself to take Zeb's heavy cock on my lips.

"Don't take him in your mouth," Ezra said. "Lick him only, we don't want you biting down from the pain."

Zeb shifted his knees apart to accommodate me, purring deep in his chest and making me yearn to do more than lick. But I didn't dare disobey Ezra while he held the crop.

"Good boy," Ezra said. He leaned in and planted a gentle kiss between my shoulder blades. "Are you ready? Remember that if it's too much you can tell me to stop."

"Yes, Master," I murmured, then went back to licking at Zeb.

Without warning, Ezra brought the crop down on my rear and I jolted, crying out. "Aah!"

The blow was a smarting, stinging thing that set my heart racing and quickly melted into pure pleasure, heat radiating out from where it had landed.

"How's it feel?" Ezra murmured, rubbing the roughness of his palm over the skin he'd whipped.

"G-good," I managed. "More, please."

Then I tried to concentrate again on licking Zeb. The second blow with the crop distracted me again, as I lost myself to the curious sensation of pain turning into pleasure. I leaned by cheek against Zeb's thigh, taking a moment to catch my breath before licking him again.

"More than five, I think," Ezra said, although I could hardly hear him over Zeb's moans.

My rear was smarting and the skin felt like it was glowing with heat from the whipping. Almost as if I was blushing down there. Some masochistic part of me didn't want it to stop.

I understood now, in the back of my mind, why Ezra had said this could be a tension release. My body tensed with each blow, physically, and then as my cells translated the sting into carnal pleasure, my body felt as if it was melting into the bed.

As Ezra continued, varying the landing of his blows from my rear to my thighs and back again, I ceased being able to think of too much at all. I simply focused on licking Zeb and pushing my ass up for Ezra to use as he would.

Eventually, I wasn't sure how long had passed, or how many times he'd struck me, he set the crop to the side and I felt his hands rubbing over my tender skin.

I moaned over Zeb's cock. Zeb, for his part, was dripping, and I was licking it up as fast as I could. Zeb seemed to understand that he shouldn't come without permission, and I admired his fortitude. I was sure without the leather around me, I would have come hard already from the rough treatment and the licking of Zeb. I could feel his arousal pulsing against my tongue, seeping into me and enhancing my own.

Ezra pushed my legs apart and soon he was stretching me with oiled fingers. I felt sweat beading on my forehead as my orgasm built but was held back from release. I groaned loudly.

Zeb pushed his cock into my mouth and I took it greedily.

Above me, I felt Ezra lean in and heard him kissing Zeb

above me. I moaned ever louder. I wished I could see all of this, that I could be enjoying it and watching it at the same time.

"Come when you need to," Ezra murmured to Zeb and with a deep moan, Zeb came almost instantly. I swallowed hard, trying not to let any spill from my mouth, as I didn't want to waste any. Almost choking on the amount of it, I swallowed again and again and licked him clean.

"That's good, both of you," Ezra said. He wrapped an arm around my waist and hauled me upright, pushed himself up into me as he settled me in his lap, my knees falling wide to the sides as Zeb watched, his eyes half hooded still.

I wasn't sure what to do with my hands in front of me, until Ezra gripped my arms, lifted them around Zeb's head and pulled him close.

Our mouths crashed together and I felt Zeb licking the taste of himself from my mouth. I groaned, mouth widening as I let him explore me, as Ezra shoved harder into me at the same moment. His cock filling me, his hips pushing against the hot, tender skin of my ass and thighs pushed me ever closer to the feeling of orgasm, although of course it was still held back.

Then the three of us were moving together, Ezra fucking into me, Zeb and I kissing, my hands moving to knead into the skin of his shoulder and whimpering into his mouth. Zeb purring loud against my chest.

Ezra gasped in my ear, his arm tight around my waist, keeping me upright and tight against him.

"Want to come, pet?"

I broke the kiss and half turned my head, wincing as Zeb bit my earlobe with surprisingly sharp teeth. My traitorous, no, *wondrous* body turned this sensation into arousal as well.

I felt like a great river dam, holding back the force of a huge raging river.

Did I want to come? Release the incredible pressure within me?

"God, yes, please," I said. "Please, Master, please, I'm so ready."

"Mmm," Ezra leaned in to snatch a kiss from the side of my mouth and then I felt his other hand between us. He tugged the leather cord, so for a moment it was tighter still and I whined loudly, then it came free and my breath hitched.

Ezra's hand closed around my cock and Zeb's at the same time. With a smooth motion he dragged his hand over the two of us, and the friction almost killed me. I couldn't come without his permission, and I managed to hold it back, although I wasn't sure I was still breathing. I was speaking but it was nothing more than a slurred, repeated plea for release.

"Please, please, please, please... p-please."

Ezra grunted, his thrusts getting more violent and erratic, pounding my tender skin. "Now, pet, come!"

I did so with a loud, whimpering cry. Tears sprung to my eyes and Zeb pushed his forehead into my neck and groaned as he came to completion as well. Finally Ezra, possibly spurred on by my spasming, squeezing body, filled me as well.

I leaned back against his chest, pulling Zeb with me, and the three of us came to a stop, all of us panting hard.

Ezra's hand moved behind Zeb to undo the buckles on the arm binder. The movements teased at me, as Ezra's rapidly softening cock shifted inside me and caused my heart to skip a few beats as I tried to catch my breath.

Once his arms were free, Zeb slipped one arm around me and with the other, stroked my chest and waist, up to caress my neck where the collar was. He kissed me softly and I whined, feeling Ezra lift me off himself and set me on my knees on the bed.

I broke the kiss to give Ezra a longing look, still pleading with him. Although we had all come I felt the need for more, the intensity of the build up was still shooting through my muscles, and I tugged against the cuffs on my wrists just to feel it, to enhance the tug inside me.

Zeb ducked out from under my arms and laid back on the pillows, panting.

Ezra fished some keys out from the bag and undid the padlocks on my cuffs, rubbed my wrists gently. "Are you all right?"

"More," I managed to breathe. "Please, Sir..."

"Mm," Ezra pulled me closer and pressed his hand on my chest. It was a curiously comforting gesture. "Tell me what you need, pet."

I leaned against his chest with my shoulder and took a deep breath. What did I need? Was it just this, just the feel of him against me? Or was it another orgasm?

"Here." Ezra moved me between him and Zeb, and although there was barely space on the bed, I was half draped over Zeb and half jammed against Ezra's chest, it should have felt uncomfortable, but it felt secure there. The warmth of both of their bodies warming me through.

Inexplicably, I felt tears welling up in my throat and a deep, shuddering tremble went through my body. Ezra put his arm around my waist and pillowed his head on his other arm. Zeb half turned and wrapped his arm around me too, pressing his chest to mine and purring gently.

They're looking after me, I thought wildly. *I don't need it, I'm making too much of a fuss. I'm being ridiculous and weak just like everyone thinks I am.*

"It's all right," Zeb said, his voice low. "You're with us, we're your family, we're yours."

Ezra placed soft kisses on the back of my shoulder. "It's a lot, pet. That was sort of the point. There's no shame in letting it out."

I swallowed, but the lump in my throat hurt now, and everything seemed to crash down around me. The fear, the sadness, the intensity of the sex. I closed my eyes, tucked my head under Zeb's chin and sobbed.

I could feel my body shaking with it, my hand curling to dig my nails into Zeb's chest.

I hated reacting like this - what if Ezra thought I hadn't enjoyed it?

I had, I had felt wonderful for a few moments there. More than wonderful. But now it felt as if that feeling had been ripped away and I was sadder than before.

I couldn't understand it.

Ezra continued to press his hand against my chest, and Zeb wrapped himself further around me. The solidity of both men, and their softly murmured reassurances finally had an effect and I calmed enough to stop crying and catch my breath.

My body still trembled and I felt slightly afraid of my own reaction, but I was able to lift my head, clear my throat and croak out "Thank you."

"It's all right, pet," Ezra said once more. He kissed my shoulder. "I pushed you, and I did it on purpose, this release at the end, that's part of it too. You did so well."

I felt the trembles ease a little at his words. I wanted to please him, and I had. That felt good.

"You, too, Zeb." Ezra reached up to run his fingers over Zeb's head and caress the black pointed ears pricking through his hair. "Now, please tell us why you have cat ears?"

Zeb shrugged. "Because you were the boss cat, I think." he mumbled. I realised his eyes were closing and he was snuggling in as if to fall asleep.

Ezra retrieved the collar from around Zeb's neck, then the one from mine. I suppressed the urge to whimper as he took it. I wanted to stay his, somehow.

As if he could hear my thoughts, he kissed my neck and stroked my hair. "Still mine, pet," he said. "But I can't sleep squashed against the wall like this."

He extricated himself from the bed and draped the blanket over the both of us.

I watched as he gathered up the various bits and pieces and put them back in the sack. He pulled his trousers back on, kissed my forehead and bade us goodnight.

Zeb was already gently snoring when the door to the cabin closed, and it didn't take long for the soft, regular noise to lull me to sleep. That, and the warmth of him slowly enveloped me, soothing my overstimulated body into rest.

Although, I think the last thought I had before I went to sleep was of Tate, and how he might feel being deprived both his regular bedfellows. My heart hurt, but I was already too drowsy - and too tangled in Zeb - to do anything about it.

CHAPTER FIFTEEN - IN WHICH GIDEON HAS SOME IMPORTANT CONVERSATIONS

J was back in Solomon's lair, sitting on the old chaise, chains around my ankles, and looking up at him as he taunted me. The sea witch stood tall and gaunt, his skin tinged with grey and eerily pearlescent in some spots. He wore only black pants, and his chest was slim but muscled.

How did I get here? I don't remember...

"Think you got away safely, don't you? Think this is over? Stupid." He spat on the ground at my feet. "This isn't over. I will not cease my work until I have Tate here, under my heel, begging for forgiveness."

He lunged forward and bared his teeth, which were long and pointed, needle thin. He was going to bite me!

I gasped and startled awake.

The morning light hit my face at an odd angle, and I looked around, confused, until I realised that I was in my own, old cabin and not tucked up with Tate as per usual.

Zeb, it seemed, had held me all night, and I smiled at the thought of that. I was uncommonly warm and my sleep had been deep. If it hadn't been for that nightmare at the end and my now wildly beating heart, I'd have felt quite serene.

Zeb wrapped his arms tighter around me and grumbled, the message quite clear - *come here and go back to sleep.*

"It's morning, Zeb," I said. I lifted his arm off me and he grumbled again but curled tightly on his side and continued to snore.

I climbed out of bed and washed my face and hands. My clothes were all in Tate's rooms now, so I pulled on the outfit from yesterday and went out on deck.

I went to find Tate. I felt I owed him an apology, or at least, to accept his from yesterday.

In the morning light, I accepted that while the circumstances hadn't been ideal, he was my Captain and I should have trusted his judgement.

After all, Tate and the crew had a lot more experience battling the Royal Fleet than I did. A lot more.

Tate was seated in his cabin, eating an apple and studying a map. I knocked on the open door and walked in, clearing my throat in case he somehow hadn't heard the knock.

He looked up and seemed to tense. His hand flattened on the map and his chewing stopped.

"Good morning," I said.

"Gideon," he said. He set the apple down and stood up from the desk.

"I uh, I wanted to," I started. "I wanted to tell you I forgive you and that I understand why you did what you did yesterday," I said. "And moreover, I'm sorry for being such a... Such a brat about the whole thing."

Tate's shoulders slumped and he moved towards me, wrapping me in a bear hug so tight he lifted me off the ground.

"I missed you last night," he muttered into my hair. I put my arms around his neck and hung on tight.

"I love you," I whispered into the hair of his chest, nosing under his shirt where it hung open. "And I'm sorry. Did you, uh, did you send Ezra?"

"I might have," Tate said. He set me down again and kissed me squarely before continuing, I kept my arms around his waist. "Had a hunch it might help."

"It did, actually," I said. "Ezra's... Ezra cares more than he lets on, I think, and he's beginning to show it a little more."

Tate shook his head. "I don't think anyone could have that effect on him but you. I love you, Gideon."

We kissed again, softly, and more and more, lingering until there was a shout from outside.

"Where's Gideon?!" I heard someone shout.

"Is that Shem?" Tate asked. I shook my head.

"No, it's Ora." I went out to the deck to find Ora, dripping wet and stark naked running towards me.

The crew were largely used to Ora by now, and few gave them a second glance in their natural state.

I instinctively reached out to catch Ora in my arms and pull them towards me, my heart thundering with fear for them.

"Are you all right, Ora?" Tate asked.

"Yes," Ora said. Then they shook their head. "No. not really. I can't -" they took a deep shuddering breath and looked me in the eyes. "I'm all right but, perhaps... perhaps I can't go back into the water for a while."

"Did you see something?" I asked. My heart thumped in my chest. My mind awhirl with all the myriad things they could have seen down there.

Sea monsters, a witch's familiars, warlike merfolk who didn't take kindly to strangers, sharks, more Naval ships. Giant crabs...

Ora swallowed and looked at Tate and then back at me. "Yes. I shouldn't... it's nothing for you to worry about. It's my business, but... I'm glad to see you. I wanted to see you."

Ora pressed their cheek against mine and I wrapped my arms tight around them. I wanted to protect Ora from anything that could make them afraid.

Tate patted Ora's back. "Get inside the cabin, I'm sure a dry towel would help," Tate said. "I'll uh, I'll give you some space."

I led Ora into the cabin and wrapped them in one of Tate's uncommonly large towels, rubbing them down through the soft fabric.

"I don't mind being damp," Ora protested, but I shook my head.

"I mind you getting the bedclothes wet," I said. "Besides, doesn't it feel good? Just let me take care of you a little."

Ora submitted to the drying off and even managed a little smile.

I reflected how grateful I was for the good sleep I'd had, for if this had happened last night when I was still a confusion of emotions I wasn't sure how well I could look after someone else. But this morning it seemed easy and natural. It made my heart warmer to give Ora this care.

I rubbed the towel in Ora's hair until they were giggling softly and their curls were a mass of frizz, and then showed them how it looked in my looking glass. I stripped off my clothes and we bundled into bed together.

Facing Ora, my chest against their shoulder, I wound my arms around them and kissed their face, pressing my skin against Ora's and felt the coolness of it against my warm skin.

"What did you see?" I asked, softly.

Ora shook their head. "I don't want to worry you further," they said. "It will probably amount to nothing."

My stomach turned uneasily but I didn't push Ora any further. "It's a strange morning," I said. "I dreamed of Solomon."

"You did?" Ora turned, lying on their side to look me in the eyes, their expression even more concerned. "Didn't Joseph dream of Solomon?"

I frowned, thinking back to that horrible day when Joseph had tried to take over the ship, using borrowed magic from the sea witch to entrance the crew of the Kelpie and try to hex me with some sort of foul, dark magic.

"He did say something like that," I said. "But this dream... It didn't feel like Solomon was trying to turn me, or get me to betray Tate. Really, he was just taunting me."

"Could still be a bad sign," Ora said. "Dark magic is dark magic. What's the purpose of visiting you in a dream just to taunt you?"

"Well, I mean. It could have just been a dream," I said, as well. "You know, a random dream."

"Did it feel real?" Ora turned their head to kiss the inside of my arm, where it was pillowing their head.

I closed my eyes and thought back. Already the memory of the dream was fading a little.

"I don't know," I said. "Yes, it felt like a real place, but that's because I was dreaming of a real place, and it was just like when I was there as a prisoner. Before I met you. So it could have just been memory. Don't dreams always feel real when you have them?"

"Maybe." Ora kissed my nose and I chuckled, opening my eyes. "But if it happens again, let me know."

"All right." I leaned in to kiss them gently on the mouth. "How are you feeling now? Safe?"

"Yes," Ora said. "Safe here with you. And Tate and the others, on the ship."

I frowned, thinking of how unsafe the ship had felt last night. The battle and the firing and my not knowing who was alive and who was dead. "I was afraid I'd lose you in the battle last night," I said. "I hated not knowing what was happening." I closed my eyes and pressed my forehead against Ora's.

Their arms tightened around me. "You'd know," they said. "You and I are linked, somehow. If I died, you'd know, just as I'd know if you did."

A shiver went down my spine and I sighed, it sounded like madness in a way, but I also felt the truth of it, I believed them. "What was it like?"

"It wasn't like a regular fight," Ora said. "The guns and the noise, it was frightening, but it was all right because we won."

I tried to imagine what it must be like to be used to being half a fish a lot of the time and then find yourself on a ship's deck. The noise and the smell of the cannons, the distant ship and somehow you had to be victorious?

"And afterwards?"

"Afterwards was strange, we sailed away so fast. I uh, I saw you, but I knew you didn't want to see me, so I went in the water and ate... uh, some of the-"

"It's all right," I said. I put my finger on their lips. "I don't need to know."

The less I thought about *that*, the better.

Ora pursed their lips and kissed the tip of my finger, and then all thoughts of what (or who) Ora ate were gone.

We were here together in bed, with nothing we had to do immediately.

I shifted closer, slipped my hand behind Ora's head and kissed them softly. "Will you let me take care of you?" I asked, softly.

Ora shook their head very slightly. "You already did, Gideon, I don't need more than that."

I smiled and leaned in to rub my nose against Ora's.

My heart was full and content, and I took a deep breath, feeling utterly contented for the first time since the ship's alarm bell had rung.

There's nothing easier than being with Ora, I thought. *I am theirs, and they are mine, and together we make a simple kind of sense. It's as comfortable as being on my own.*

We fell asleep together then, I'm not sure how much Ora had slept, but I stroked their hair and they dozed off quickly. I didn't want to move, it was too warm and too comfortable there, so I drifted off, too.

The rest of the day and night was uneventful, although I chose to sleep in my cabin again - not because I was still angry with Tate exactly, but because a little space felt right. Ora went back into the bowsprit netting and Ezra slept in his hammock.

Zeb found me and pressed himself against me, covering my back with his broad chest and wrapping his arms around me. I used his arm as a pillow, and we slept tangled together like that, like one being almost.

Being with Zeb was becoming easier, too. As I adjusted to his eccentric ways, well, they were only eccentric if you compared them to someone who had been a human their entire lives. I had become used to his ways, and I loved him.

The next day dawned with the ringing of the alarm bell.

CHAPTER SIXTEEN - IN WHICH THE KELPIE RUNS

The bell woke me with a start. I groaned, I was shoved to the side of the bed with my face pressed against the wall of the cabin. Zeb had rolled onto his back in the night and simply from the width of his shoulders had taken up most of the space in the narrow cot.

I turned and scrambled over him, not being too careful. If there was going to be another battle I wanted to be a part of it this time, or at least, I wanted to see what was there before Tate stowed me in his cabin again.

I pulled on my trousers and opened my cabin door to see the crew emerging from below deck. Sagorika was ringing the bell.

"Naval ship!" she cried.

A hand closed on my shoulder and I turned to see Ezra, his face bleary with sleep. "Come on," he said, wearily.

I nodded and followed him to Tate's cabin, just as Tate bellowed from the helm. "Anchor up! Full sail!"

"Oh?" Ezra said. "Apparently, we're going to run.'

I swallowed, looking to the East and seeing the Royal ship some leagues away but clearly heading towards us.

Ezra let go of my shoulder and we watched as members of the crew scaled the rigging and unfurled the sails. Shem, James and two others were hauling the anchor up and soon the ship was flying, skimming waves. The wind on the deck increased.

Tate strode past Ezra and me.

"Must've approached in the night," Tate muttered. Ezra fell into step beside him and I hurried to follow. "Why are they targeting us?"

"Perhaps they know we sunk the last one?" Ezra said. His usually confident tone was tentative. Not quite diffident, but not challenging either.

Tate groaned in purest frustration, raked both hands through his hair and then dropped his arms to his sides. He glanced at me and huffed his breath out in a ragged sigh.

"Your father might've upped the orders, or increased the reward for your return," he said.

"If he's done that, how could he have... how would they have got the news?" I asked. "Surely out here the ship would've already been at sea, and pigeons can't get this far..."

"There's rumours," Ezra said. He tapped a finger on his chin, eyes narrowed, staring at the ship in the distance. "Some Naval ships take on a witch for communication. They can send messages through eldritch means. I don't know if it's true but."

"I've heard that too," Tate said. "They say a ship with a witch on it has all sorts of advantages."

I frowned. If it was true, it was certainly bad news for us.

"The Grey Kelpie is known as a privateer," Tate continued. "But any amount of investigation would show I never received a letter of Marque. We may scrape by as a merchantman, if they boarded us, but only if you were nowhere to be seen."

My stomach fell and I felt the blood drain from my face. If

Father had increased the reward, then it made sense that more Naval ships would be out searching, but it meant we had to worry about other ships as well - privateers and other pirates. Many would be looking to claim that bounty.

I stopped walking, closed my eyes and silently cursed my father's name, wrapped my arms around my chest against the sudden chill I felt from within.

The ship was moving quickly now, the wind whipped at my hair and I could feel the surge of waves beneath us. The sun on my cheeks felt warm and I reflected it would be a beautiful day for sailing if there wasn't such a threat to us.

I felt arms slip around me and inhaled, it was Ora, I recognised their scent.

"It's all right, Gideon," Ora said, softly, right into my ear.

I opened my eyes and bit my lip. "It's not though, this is my fault."

Tate was at the stern, his spyglass in hand, staring in the direction of the Naval ship. "It's pursuing!" he called.

Zeb ambled onto the deck. "What's all the fuss about?" He asked, through a yawn.

"Anything we don't need in the hold can be dumped overboard!" Tate shouted as he stomped back up the deck.

"Right," I said.

Finally, I could be of some use.

"There are some boxes below, I know which ones aren't necessary. Come on." Zeb and Ora followed me down to the place I'd found the crates of seemingly random goods when I'd been hiding from my desires and working to catalogue the ship's chattels.

It was hard work, heaving the half dozen or so boxes up the

stairs and onto the deck, even with all three of us working to balance them between us.

Zeb complained, grumbling that he was accustomed to humans doing the hard work. "You should do this while I watch," he said.

Shaking my head, I snapped at him. "This is an emergency, you heard the Captain!"

He rolled his eyes, but he helped and didn't grumble any more.

I had no idea how useful it was, given the boxes weren't exactly heavy, but it felt good to be doing something.

Sagorika approached as we stacked the last crate on the deck. "We can toss these, Quartermaster," I said. "With your permission. This one has a vase, those ones are clothes and the others have some dolls in them"

Sagorika gave them a glance and then nodded. "Yes, over the side."

Two other crew members - Anton and James - helped us to push the crates over the side of the ship.

"The wind's with us," James said, looking up at the sails as we dusted off our hands.

I went to the stern to look behind us. We were outpacing the Naval galleon. It was a large ship, and would be hard to turn. The Grey Kelpie was a smuggling ship, built for speed and agility, so we had that advantage. Especially as Tate had been so quick to order the sails out.

"They're not on our wind," Tate said, appearing beside me. He handed me the spyglass and gripped the wooden rails with both hands. I looked through it and found the ship.

I stared at it through the glass. It was too distant, and on the wrong angle to see the name painted on the sides, but some part of me thought it looked like my old ship - the Naval ship I'd served on for less than a year.

My heart thumped and I gave the glass back to Tate. His knuckles were white on the railing.

"We have to find somewhere they won't find us," he muttered.

I swallowed. The British Navy was dominant on the seas - how could you avoid something so ubiquitous? I didn't have the fortitude to say as much to Tate.

"How would you normally, uh, achieve that?" I asked, hesitantly.

He sighed, rubbed his hand over his beard and then dropped his hand back down again. "Tortuga, Splintered Isles... neither of those places seem particularly friendly at the moment. So maybe North and West towards the Bahamas, we should be able to hide there..." he glared down the spyglass at the Naval ship and then stuffed it into the pocket of his waistcoat.

Then he turned and shouted more orders.

By a little after noon everyone's tempers were getting frayed. The ship pursuing us had vanished over the horizon a couple of hours earlier, but it felt good to continue to sail as fast as possible and get more distance between us and them.

Ezra was at the helm. Tate had continued to pace up and down the ship, offering help or assistance when needed, making sure no one had a question that hadn't been answered.

After the exertions of the morning with the crates - and Tate snapping at him for being in the way - Zeb had taken to bed in my old cabin.

Ora and I had gone to work with the rest of the crew, adjusting lines and generally helping to make sure the ship was running as best it could.

It was hard work, and work I was out of practise in. Even during my year in the Navy I'd felt ill-suited to keep up the pace the other sailors seemed able to maintain.

I should do this more, so I can be of more use. Then maybe Tate won't insist I wait in the cabin next time we're attacked.

My hands were soon smarting from handling the taut ropes. My back ached and I was sure my skin was sunburned. I'd had to tie my hair back to keep it off my neck, but it was finding its way free all the same, clinging in unpleasant tendrils to my face.

My shirt was soaked with sweat and, generally, it was hard work. I felt less glad to do it the more the hours wore on. Tate had created an atmosphere of urgency, which was frightening in some way, my stomach in knots, and the rest of the crew on edge. Although as time wore on and his commands became fewer, the tension eased.

"We're well clear now," Anton said, finally. He'd paused to wipe the sweat off his brow. His dark hair hung limp around his temples.

"Captain's got a bee in his bonnet, that's for sure," Shem said. We all looked over to the helm where Tate gripped the wheel and stared out into the distance.

"I can talk to him," I said.

"Might be a good idea, if you can uh, relax him some," Anton said, his eyebrows raising.

"Quite," I said, clearing my throat.

Approaching the helm I licked my lips, all the fears and exertion from the day bubbling to the top of my mind.

He glanced over at me and nodded. "Gideon."

"We haven't been able to see the Naval ship for a long time," I said. "Maybe it's time you let someone else take the helm?"

"Mm," he said. "Maybe."

"Not just maybe," I said, feeling bolder since he hadn't snapped at me. "You need a rest. And a drink. And we all need some lunch."

He looked up at the rigging, stuck his fingers in his mouth and whistled shrilly. Ezra's face appeared, peering down from the crow's nest.

Tate signalled him and he nodded and started the climb down the rigging. I shuddered and tore my eyes away.

"Lunch you say?" Tate said. "I think Sagorika's on food today..."

"Shouldn't you be the one who knows that for sure?" Ezra asked, landing lightly nearby.

He must've moved between the yardarms, thank Heavens he didn't fall.

"Aye, but other things have occupied my mind," Tate said. He moved back, allowing Ezra to take the helm and hesitated, then squeezed his shoulder with one hand. Ezra smiled, briefly, just the corner of his mouth, but something around his eyes softened as well.

I smiled, seeing this moment of tenderness between them. It was progress, and it filled my heart. I kissed Ezra on the cheek and then took Tate's hand. "Come on, food. And then rest."

"Rest, is it?" Tate shook his head. "I don't think I can manage that."

"Oh, I think you can, with my help," I said. I gave him a smile and he smiled back, something tense in his eyes made me squeeze his hand.

I led him down to the galley for some food, smiling wider to myself as some ideas sprung to mind about how to relax my Captain.

CHAPTER SEVENTEEN - IN WHICH RELAXATION IS FOUND

*S*agorika had made an incredible rice and curry sauce dish, which was spicy and invigorating - something I'd not tasted before, even from the market in Kingston. We ate off plates next to the galley.

"Sagorika, you've outdone yourself," Tate said.

"Mm," Sagorika replied. "you know, if we hired a regular ship's cook you wouldn't have to lose your Quartermaster for hours at a time."

Tate grunted. "But we'd have the same boring food day in and day out. I like how everyone tries something different."

Sagorika rolled her eyes and then looked at me. "Looks like you stuck your back into it out there."

"I, uh, yes," I said. I licked my lips and took another bite of curry.

"Maybe soon I can show you a bit about how the ship works in battle?" Sagorika looked at Tate, as if she was afraid he'd contradict her. He looked between us and then shrugged.

"Couldn't hurt."

"Oh. I'd love that," I said. "Then I could actually help."

"If the Navy gets close again, I'm still going to hide you," he said. "But I agree. You'd best learn as much as you can about the ship."

Sagorika winked at me.

She must've noticed how grumpy I was and figured out the solution. I should've come and asked her in the first place.

Tate seemed to relax once there was food in his belly, and didn't object when I suggested we retire to his cabin.

Zeb had appeared, sniffing around the kitchen as we finished up eating, so I was confident that we'd have Tate's cabin - and bed - to ourselves.

I closed the door behind us and Tate turned, watching me, from the centre of the room. I looked at him, not hesitating so much as allowing myself a moment to admire him. Even sweat-soaked and weary as I felt, I wanted him with a fierce passion.

"I take it this means I'm forgiven?" Tate asked, finally.

My back straightened and I cleared my throat. "I already forgave you," I said.

"You said you did, and then you slept in your old cabin again last night," he said. He shrugged off his waistcoat and tossed it in a corner - Tate's way of signalling that an item of clothing needed cleaning.

"I did," I said. "I didn't mean to do it to punish you, or, perhaps I did on some level. It just... felt like what I needed."

Tate nodded and folded his arms over his chest. "Well, what now?"

"Now." I crossed to the pitcher of water and basin kept in the corner. I checked inside the jug and was pleased to find it close to full. I hadn't refilled it that morning so it must still be the water from the day before. That would do. "Now we wash."

"Wash?" Tate laughed. "Just when I think you can't surprise me again, Gideon, you do something totally unexpected."

I shrugged and pulled my shirt off, setting it to one side.

"Come on, clothes off too," I said, briskly. Tate chuckled and stripped off his shirt, it clung to his biceps and his back, plastered on with sweat and salt air.

The sight of his tan back, all those muscles and tribal tattoos carved into his skin - I felt myself get harder. But I was determined to relax him.

I found a washcloth, tipped some water into the basin and dipped the cloth in.

"Come sit," I said. He tugged over the nearest chair and sat, looking bemused.

I started to wash him with the damp cloth, rubbing gently and rinsed the sweat and salt off his skin.

This is another thing I've never done before, I thought idly. *Washing a body that isn't mine. It's far more intimate than I'd imagined.*

Tate's shoulders relaxed as I washed him, his muscles slowly unknotting under my hands, and I leaned in and kissed him as I cleaned him. He hummed a soft tune as I worked, something I'd never heard before.

"That's lovely," I said, quietly, not wanting to interrupt him but curious at the same time.

"My mother used to sing it," he said.

"What was she like?" I asked, smiling. Memories of my own mother were always happy ones, aside from at the end.

"She was... Well, she hated London," he said. "Father met her when he served in the Navy, she was from an island in the South Pacific. They fell in love and he brought her to London, but she hated the cold."

I nodded a little. "I couldn't imagine living somewhere cold after Jamaica," I said.

"She taught me the songs of her people, the stories... strange fables my father said were blasphemous. More than one god, spirits walking the Earth, creation occurring by accident... That kind of thing. I liked them, though."

I picked up his arm in one hand and rubbed the damp cloth down it, caressing his biceps and watching his face. He had a dreamy smile and his eyes were crinkled. I leaned in to kiss him on the mouth.

After the kiss, he looked at me. "How about your mother, Gideon? I've seen the picture in your cabin."

"Mother was..." I shrugged a little and smiled. "She was the sun, to me. She was everything. Good and kind, and with her around my father wasn't cruel, he was... fun even. But when she died, he stopped everything. He couldn't stand the sight of me any more, he couldn't laugh or do anything but be angry."

"My mother died, too." Tate took my hand in his and squeezed it. "Influenza. Da passed soon after. I was fifteen."

"Is that when you joined the Navy?" I squeezed his hand back and then shifted to wash his other arm, then moved my ministrations to his chest, which was more intimate still. My breath was becoming heavy.

"Aye, it was."

He watched me with a soft expression I couldn't read, but it spoke to me on a deeper level. My heart recognised it and it resonated in my chest, the loss and the pain.

"I'm sorry you lost them," I said.

Tate shook his head. "It was a long time ago, and they wouldn't approve of what I'm doing now. In a way, I'm glad they're gone, so they didn't have to learn about my bad behaviour."

I think Mother understands what I'm doing. But of course, Father would never accept it. If he knew.

"I'm sorry about your mother," he said, then.

"Thank you," I said. I dipped the cloth into the basin and brought it, dripping, to his chest. He shivered as the water ran down his chest and spilled onto his trousers. "Oh dear, clumsy of me."

"Very clumsy indeed. Almost not like you, Gideon. I suppose I'll have to take them off, since they're so wet," Tate said.

I laughed softly, then kissed him and he slipped his hand around my waist, pulled me in closer against him. He took the cloth from me and dripped water down my bare back, making me shiver, and giggle with surprise.

Tate laughed as I tried to pull away, he pulled me into his lap and dipped the cloth again, returning the favour and cleaning me off - albeit in a much more slapdash manner, as I was kissing him with more and more fervour.

"Your trousers," I managed to say finally.

"Mm." Tate wrapped his arms around me and stood, lifting me in his arms as if I weighed nothing, and carried me to the bed. He set me down and pulled my trousers off, running his hands over my hips and waist and making a soft noise of need before straightening up to remove his own.

Then he leapt on top of me, making me laugh again, his large, hard body crushing me into the bed in the most delicious way. I wound my arms around him.

"What do you want, love?" Tate murmured, kissing my neck as I arched under him. The friction of him rubbing against me felt like all I needed, my mind blanked on any other response.

"Just this, just... You," I gasped. "Please."

"Inside you, or do you want to fuck me?" He bit the skin of my throat so gently I shivered with the tiny prick of pain.

"I- I don't mind, whatever you want," I said, closing my eyes.

Tate chuckled. "All right, how about I ride you, then?" He licked at my collarbone and I shuddered bodily.

"Good Lord, yes."

He sat up, retrieving the coconut oil pot and settling with his knees on either side of my hips. I stroked my hands over his chest and down, pressing my fingers in to feel each muscle, each hard line that led me down to his gorgeous cock, which was sitting out from his body, hard and ready. I curled my head forward to lick the tip of it, pleased that his thighs were so large I wasn't utterly bending myself in half to do it.

Tate moaned deep in his chest and I slid my hands up to tease his nipples, tugging gently on them as he teased himself open.

My cock throbbed under him, and I quickly had to give up on licking at him as I was having trouble breathing, wanting so powerfully to be inside him now that he'd promised it.

"That'll do," he murmured and used a hand to guide me to push inside him. I pushed up as best I could and he sank down, until I was buried inside him - the heat and the squeeze of him was so delicious I almost came in that instant.

Tate leaned forward, bracing his hand beside my shoulder. I linked my arms around his neck and crashed my mouth to his, kissing him with all the happiness and yearning I was feeling.

I had missed him in the two nights I'd spent apart from him, and the fact that I was now inside him, as close as two people could possibly be, was making my heart surge with joy.

Tate began to rock his hips, pulling himself almost all the way off me before sinking back down again.

It was almost too much. I let go of him and fell back against the pillow, my chest heaving with the effort of breathing. It wasn't just wonderful sensations of Tate fucking himself on me, but his weight on me - not crushing me, but adding more pressure. Making me feel like I was being used in the most inflaming way.

I pawed at his chest, ineffective, sure I couldn't possibly be doing enough to give him as much enjoyment as he was giving me.

Tate pushed up on his hand, watching my face as I panted.

I locked eyes with him, feeling the connection between us from the way I'd cleaned him, the care I'd taken of him, and the discussion we'd had about our pasts and about loss. It was all working together, compounded by the stresses of the morning and the fear of being chased, and making our lovemaking into something so intimate that tears sprung to my eyes.

"Tate," I breathed, one hand kneading into his chest.

"I'm here, love, I'm with you," Tate whispered. His voice hoarse and thick with need.

I slipped my hand down to stroke his cock and his breath caught, I saw it happen in the hitch of his chest and the movement of his throat as he swallowed hard.

I saw him so clearly, his heart and his soul, and I felt like I'd burst with the strength of love I had for him.

"I love you so much, so much," I gasped.

He sped up the movements of his hips, I wanted more then, more control of the movements. I let go of his cock and tugged on his hips.

"Roll over," I said. "Onto your back."

He wrapped both arms around me and rolled us, balancing me on top of him and I sighed with relief, rocking my hips into him and stroking his cock with my hand.

His body, laid out under me was one of the most beautiful, most incendiary sights I had ever seen - gorgeous enough I almost felt I should avert my eyes, like seeing an angel and their bright, holy light.

I gasped and closed my eyes, feeling my orgasm nearing.

"With me," Tate said, his hands gripping my hips and making me fuck into him harder and faster still.

I pumped my hand over his cock. The moment of completion neared and it was as if I could taste it on my tongue. Tate's chest heaving and my own breathing ragged, matching the same rhythm. I locked eyes with him again and we came in the same instant, bucking and crying out, gazing into each other as if we could see each other's souls.

I felt my skin prickling and a coolness wash over me like there was a cool breeze in the room. The quality of light in the room turned soft and golden, and I found I couldn't look away from Tate's eyes. I didn't want to, even if I had been able to.

In that moment, it felt like I saw everything that he was and had been. Then something snapped up between us, and the spell was broken.

It was a heady feeling, as if I'd drunk too much champagne too quickly, and I fell forward onto his chest, giggling.

Tate wrapped his arms around me and held me as he caught his breath. I let the mirth run out of me in laughter until I was able to sigh and relax, shifting my hips to withdraw from him, and the two of us lay there, our breathing perfectly synchronised.

After some long, contented minutes, Tate shifted under me. "That was... something else," he said.

"Mmm," I said. I lifted my head enough to kiss his neck. "You're wonderful."

"No, you're the wonderful one," I said. "I'm sorry I was so petty, and that I didn't sleep in here last night."

His chest rumbled and he squeezed me. "Forgiven."

"I need to check our course," he said, and I grumbled, but rolled off him, got up and retrieved the damp cloth and cleaned him off before helping him into his clothes. My head spun a little, and I became aware of a bone deep weariness in my body. Whatever had happened between us, it had taken a toll on me.

"I might stay here, and nap," I said, before yawning so wide my jaw clicked. I blinked it away and smiled.

"You do that." Tate watched as I got back into bed then pulled the blanket over me. Although it was plenty warm in the cabin, I appreciated the gesture. He leaned in and kissed me softly.

"Thank you, Gideon," he said, his voice soft with something like wonder. "I feel so much better now. My mind is clear."

I smiled, turned on my side and watched him leave the cabin. I wondered why he'd thanked me, or why he thought sex would have cleared his head...

I suppose it does put things into perspective, and besides, it feels so good, most other things don't seem to matter so much.

I was asleep in a moment. And that's when I dreamed of Solomon again.

CHAPTER EIGHTEEN - IN WHICH THE KELPIE IS BECALMED

I stood beside Solomon on the edge of a cliff. It seemed perfectly natural that I would be there with him, my mind wasn't concerned about the how of it, no, it was utterly focused on the dreadful fall in front of me.

Although I knew it would make me more frightened, I couldn't resist dropping my eyes to look at the sheer drop. It was dizzyingly high. My feet were so close to the edge of the cliff. If I curled my toes I would feel the place where the ground ceased and gave way to thin air.

I was aware I was dressed in my old Naval uniform.

The stiff leather of the boots that had never quite broken in. The high collar scratching my neck. The shiny brass buttons on my jacket catching the sunlight. I adjusted the way my jacket sat at my waist.

Seagulls cried out and the sound of the sea was distant to my ears.

Far away, what felt like miles below us, waves crashed on large rocks. If one was to fall from here, one would meet their end on those jagged rocks.

I couldn't breathe, my chest was tight, and all I wanted was to back away, but I couldn't move. No matter how I tried, how much I wanted it, I couldn't make my body move.

"It's easy really," Solomon said. "All you have to do is believe in the power within you. Draw it up, like water from a well, and then you can do this..."

I sensed his movement beside me and it drew my eye. He took a step forward, out into the air.

"No!" Instinctively, I lunged to grab him - pull him back to safety. But I had forgotten how close to the edge I was.

My booted foot plunged into the air.

My hand grasped at Solomon's long, tattered cloak and for a moment I thought he would buoy me up, that I could hang onto him and not fall, but the fabric slipped through my fingers, the wind rushed in my ears and I was falling, screaming as the waves rushed towards me.

My entire body jolted and I sat up, panting.

I was in bed. In bed in Tate's cabin.

I was safe. I couldn't fall off a cliff from bed.

I took a deep breath, feeling it fill my lungs like I hadn't breathed properly for a while.

From the angle of the sun coming through the window it seemed to be late afternoon so I got up, washed myself again - sweat from the dream, and from Tate and I enjoying each other. I got dressed and went out on deck.

The ship was still sailing at a fine clip, but the mood on the ship had relaxed. Sagorika was sitting with Zeb and they were laughing about something.

Tate was inspecting a cannon with Ezra, their faces both serious and focused.

I went looking for Ora, checked the bowsprit netting and

found them lying naked, basking in the sun and the sea spray, eyes closed - possibly asleep.

Everyone seemed busy.

No one needs me.

I ignored the whiny voice in the back of my head and swallowed down the sudden fear that I was superfluous.

What is wrong with me? Why do I need to be noticed, or given attention so much? Am I really that insecure about everything?

I shook my head and went to my cabin to look at my portrait of Mother. It seemed only right after talking about her with Tate earlier. Especially since I was apparently disappointed that I hadn't been mobbed with attention as soon as I'd walked out on deck.

"Mother, I'm absolutely ridiculous," I said, sitting down. "One bad dream and I want all the comfort and attention from everyone, even though they all have their own jobs and things."

I rubbed my fingers up from the bridge of my nose to my forehead, sighing mightily. Something stirred in the back of my head.

"Only, it wasn't one dream, was it? I had one the other day as well..." My stomach sank with a nauseous feeling. "And Joseph... Solomon visited him in dreams and he went utterly evil, controlled by Solomon remotely somehow."

I stood up. "Sorry, Mother, I'd better let the others know right away, this could be a very bad sign. I'll talk to you later."

I gave her a wave and went back out, heading towards where Tate and Ezra had been earlier. Now Tate was standing back, watching as Ezra lay on his back partially under the cannon, one leg bent, the other stretched out on the deck.

My ridiculously enthusiastic libido instantly wondered what would happen if I pulled Ezra's trousers and open and started licking at him while he worked, and what Tate would say or do if I did that, but I dismissed the thought.

Not the time.

I cleared my throat and Tate looked at me. "Gideon, how was your nap?"

"Good," I said. "Well, sort of. Sort of concerning as well. I uh..." I hesitated as Ezra slid out from under the cannon, his cheek had a smudge of soot on it, and his shirt hung open.

So very handsome.

"How can a nap be concerning?" Ezra asked. He raised an eyebrow at me as he dusted his hands off on his trousers. His eyes dropped pointedly to my crotch and I cleared my throat and folded my hands in front of myself.

Pull yourself together, Gideon. Mind out of the gutter and deliver the news you have to deliver.

"I-I had a dream. But it-it wasn't just any dream, it was a dream with Solomon in it," I stammered.

"With - with... Oh." Tate's expression turned from relaxed and amused to thunderous in a second.

"And?" Ezra asked.

"He visited Joseph in his dreams, remember, and he turned evil," I wrung my hands together. All arousal drained out of me. "I don't want that to happen to me."

Tate swore and rubbed his hand over his eyes, then looked at me. "What happened in the dream?"

"I-it was... not the first time I've dreamed about him," I said, slowly. My stomach shivered in a horrid way.

Ezra stood up and looked between Tate and me. "I don't think Solomon's about to turn Gideon evil," he said. "There's not an evil bone in his body. Even if he tried, I can't imagine it working."

"You really think so?" I asked, feeling pleased despite my fears. Ezra flashed me his wolfish smile and I returned it.

"I think Solomon has more power than we can understand," Tate said. "And whatever you think of Gideon's bones, there's no telling what he can do. We're not even near the Splintered Isles for Christ's sake. He shouldn't be able to..."

Ezra raised his eyebrows and screwed his mouth to the side. "I don't understand any of this. Magic was never my forté."

"Neither," I said. "I told Ora about the first one but they said it was probably just a dream. Now that I've had another..." I sighed, dropped my hands to my sides. "It feels like a pattern. And it's frightening me."

"What happens in the dreams?"

"Uh, well..." I cleared my throat to start but Tate shook his head.

"Let's sit down first." He led the two of us to the wooden benches I'd sat on weeks ago to hear Sagorika tell the legends she knew about Solomon. But now it was my turn. I sat in the middle, Tate sat on my right side and Ezra on my left.

Their presence grounded me, stopped a little of the shivery, unpleasant feeling.

"In the first it was just like I was back in his cave," I said. "When he kidnapped me. And nothing much happened, except he said he wouldn't rest until he had you, Tate."

I put my hand on Tate's knee and he jumped, then covered my hand with his own. "I see, and today's one, was it the same?"

I shook my head, and recounted the dream in as much detail as I could remember, although the memory was getting hazy now.

"It didn't feel like he was trying to turn me evil, but he wants me to know he's still... I don't know, thinking about us? About Tate and me, anyway."

Ezra moved closer to my side and put his hand on my back. His hand felt large, steady and warm and I realised I was trembling from the recounting of the dreams.

I took a breath.

"And in his lair," Ezra said, slowly. "When he had you. In real life, I mean, what did he say then?"

I thought back to those two days. "He's obsessed with Tate," I said, finally. "He wants revenge, he's so angry. But, but under that, he was hurt, I think. There was something still human about him, something that could maybe be... be saved?"

Tate laughed, coldly. "I'd be very surprised if that was the case."

"So, why is he sending dreams to you and not Tate, then?" Ezra said. He slipped his hand around my waist and tugged me closer to him. I leaned against him, gratefully.

"I don't know, but um. I suppose there's something else I ought to tell you." I swallowed. Tate looked at me sharply and I felt my cheeks warm. "I don't know exactly what it is, or what it means, but Ora said I have some trace of something magical."

"A trace?" Ezra asked. I half turned to look at him.

"Yes, I don't understand it either. But they said, uh. They said there's something in my blood. And that we need a witch to determine, or augur I guess, what it really means."

Tate's eyebrows knotted together and he frowned. He opened his mouth to speak when there was a shout from the stern. I saw Anton waving at us.

Tate stood immediately and strode to him. Ezra and I got up and followed.

My heart was speeding up. There were no sails on the horizon, just clouds. Which were no obvious cause for alarm, only we'd just been talking about Solomon and some ill-divining part of my soul felt like this sudden call of alarm was related.

"What is it?" Tate asked, his voice gruff.

"Those clouds," Anton said. "I think it's a fog bank."

Tate swore softly, but as I looked on the clouds I saw it was likely true. The clouds were thick and a yellow, nearly brown colour, spreading fast over the water.

A creeping, prickling sensation crept from the soles of my feet up my legs and over my entire body, giving me goose pimples. This wasn't a natural fog, there was no way. Sea fog commonly came upon a ship overnight, not racing after a ship in the afternoon sunshine.

"How fast?" Tate asked.

"Matter of minutes, I think," Anton said. He tugged at the collar of his shirt.

Tate swore, hesitated a moment, staring as the fog indeed ate up the ocean and sped towards us.

"Loose the sheets! Aweigh anchor!" Tate shouted.

It was so sudden that I startled, half stumbling into Ezra who didn't move, just stuck a hand out and braced my shoulder. Possibly he'd been expecting it.

Tate stomped back up the ship, calling out orders and swearing.

All over the ship, there was movement as the ship was brought to a stop. I swallowed and looked at Ezra who was still staring at the fog.

"I really, really hate magic," Ezra murmured.

I shivered again, this time feeling a hollow open in my

stomach, since I had just confessed there was a chance I had magic in my blood somewhere - although that was unproven.

"I suppose you couldn't accept me," I found I was saying, despite myself. "If it turns out there is something in me?"

Ezra tore his gaze away from the rapidly approaching fog and looked into my eyes, penetrating deep into me in that unique way he had. I felt the connection between us almost as a physical thing, but I was afraid that it would be broken if he said the wrong thing now.

"No, Gideon. I've often felt there was something strange and unique about you, and if it's magic, then it's magic. But I suspect it's just you. Your... individual and intriguing spirit."

Oh, thank Heavens. That was a good answer.

I smiled, pushed up on my toes, bracing my hands on his chest to kiss him, smiling as his stubble grazed my chin.

"You're wonderful," I murmured against his lips. "I love you."

"I know you do," Ezra said. His voice was loaded with affection and amusement, but he didn't say the words back. In some way, I knew he needed more time. And, although it did give my heart a pang, I knew I would be happy to wait for him to get there as well.

I kissed him again, harder and then let go to see if I could help somehow. Perhaps with the dinner preparations?

CHAPTER NINETEEN - IN WHICH
ENTERTAINMENT IS FOUND

*I*t was a strange evening.

The fog muffled sound. We weren't sailing, of course, and the fog hung low over the ship, droplets of water sticking to people's eyelashes and hair, snuffing out the stars and making the moon a sort of sickly glow.

The crew were quiet. They were superstitious about the nature of the fog and what it meant. Ezra, Sagorika, Tate and I sat together to eat on the benches.

"An ill omen," Sagorika said darkly.

Ezra hushed her, and for a moment there was a flash in her eye like she was going to snap at him, but Ezra caught her eye and then looked significantly at Tate and her shoulders relaxed.

Tate was pulling his hair back into a ponytail and then immediately loosing it again. Twisting it into a curious bun and then two minutes later pulling it free. I'd never seen him fidget in such a way.

Ora had come up on deck from their net when dinner was served, and sat beside me, on the bench uncharacteristically quiet.

Zeb was stalking the perimeter of the ship, his eyes on the fog - ever watchful.

"How long does fog usually... Uh, stick around?" I asked, after a while. I'd finished up my meal of hot oat pancakes cooked by James.

"Impossible to say," Ezra said. "Sometimes it'll burn off mid morning, sometimes it hangs about for days."

Tate stood up and set his hands on his hips.

"I'm going to bed," he said. "Set a double watch tonight, Ezra, make sure they're sharp listeners. We'll deal with tomorrow when it comes."

"Aye," Ezra said. He stood up and stalked off to organise the crew into watch shifts.

"Sagorika," I said. I knew she had some magic, but I didn't know the extent of it. "Do you think there's any way you'd be able to tell if I have magical blood?"

Sagorika gave me a skeptical look. "No, son, my magic is thin at best, and mostly herbs and brews. You'd need a proper witch."

"Thank you," I said. I squeezed Ora's hand. We cleared up the plates from dinner and helped James wash them before heading back onto the deck. Zeb was nowhere in sight.

Ezra caught me looking around. "If you're after Zeb, I've put him on watch," he said. "He was already sniffing the air and stalking about, and he agreed readily enough."

"All right," I said. "I'll... I'll see you tomorrow then." I gave Ezra a kiss goodnight. Ora smiled, and then went in to do the same before Ezra realised what was happening. He didn't push them away though, and even squeezed their waist briefly before he shook his head.

"Good night, you two. Rest well."

Tate was reading one of my romance stories by candlelight when Ora and I let ourselves into the Captain's cabin, and with a little coaxing he agreed to read it aloud to the two of us.

With the blankets and the candlelight, the story, and two of my lovers sandwiching me in the bed, it was a surprisingly cosy night given the circumstances.

In the morning I woke up when Tate got up. Ora slipped out from under my arm then, too, I presumed to go linger in the net and get themselves wet. It hurt my heart a little that Ora wasn't free to swim in the ocean as they liked. They should have freedom.

I sat up in bed and hugged my knees, watching them get dressed and yawning.

"Any dreams this morning?" Tate asked as he pulled on his blue waistcoat.

I shook my head. "Not a thing."

"That's good," Ora said, they winked at me. "See you soon."

Once I was alone in the room I sat back against the pillows. I hadn't dreamed anything, but I felt a niggling in the back of my head. The question of whether or not I was magic was weighing on my mind and I wanted to explore it a little.

I thought back to the magic I'd seen before. Ora sang, but I had sung songs before and not noticed any kind of strange effects from it.

Solomon had done a lot of complicated gestures, his long fingers seeming to dance in the wind. I tried to mimic what I remembered, thinking hard about creating something from nothing.

Nothing happened.

What else could Solomon do? Oh, the weather.

I cleared my throat, thought very hard about summoning a wind, and tried a different sort of gesture, fluttering my fingers in a sort of swooping movement in front of me.

Laughter from outside the cabin door. I dropped my hands into my lap and scrambled out of bed to wash.

I didn't think anyone could have seen me do that, but I didn't want anyone to walk in on it either. I'd look a complete fool.

I pulled my trousers and shirt on and combed out my hair. There were definitely people talking nearby on the deck, Tate and Ezra's low growl. Maybe Ora, too?

Listening, I heard a couple of scraps of conversation.

"No one's moving in this weather, no wind, the thick fog..."

"Sure he'll like it?"

"Oh yes."

Flicking my hair over my shoulders, I went to the door, opening it just as Tate put his hand on the door handle.

"Oh, I'm sorry," I said, I stepped back.

"I was looking for you," Tate said.

"Well, I-I'm still in here." I was aware of how redundant this conversation was getting, I cleared my throat. "Uh, what was it you wanted?"

"You, obviously." His tone sent a thrill through me and I flushed almost instantly. I took a step back into the cabin.

"Well, if you'd been a minute or two earlier you would have caught me without clothes on," I said. I smiled and reached for his hand.

"Caught you, yes. That's what I wanted to do." He grinned wide and his eyes glinted with promise.

"I, all right?" I raised my eyebrows, confused.

"You're into it, you're not too sleepy still?" Tate took my hand but didn't follow me into the cabin. "Because well, me and the lads... we had a bit of an idea..."

The warmth in my body increased, and my cock throbbed once. Had... had they been outside talking about me?

What were they talking about?

Why me?

I opened my mouth to ask, and swallowed, feeling suddenly out of my depth.

"I, uh, I'm sorry," I said, falling back on the ridiculous levels of politeness that always kicked in when I was feeling like I didn't understand what was going on. "I'm afraid I don't quite understand."

Tate's hand tightened on mine. "Do you trust me?" There was a twinkle in his gorgeous green eyes and I swallowed.

"Yes, of course I do, Tate."

"And the others, you trust them, too?"

"I, yes. Yes, I trust all of you, otherwise I wouldn't..." I trailed off. Lord knows I'd been in enough ridiculous and frankly outlandish sexual scenarios with Tate and my other lovers, but for some reason, in that moment, with Tate looking at me rather like he wanted to devour me whole, I couldn't even say 'make love'. Thankfully he seemed to understand what I was getting at.

"All right, then follow me."

He turned and tugged me out of the cabin.

"As if I have any choice with you holding onto me like that," I muttered, but I wasn't actually angry. I had a mounting sense of anticipation as if it were about to be a holiday, or someone was throwing me a party.

They wouldn't throw me a party on the ship, would they? No. We're becalmed in a strange fog, of course they wouldn't.

The ship was still at anchor and the fog hadn't moved. The

fog filtered the morning light into a strange, cool greyness, and the only sound I could hear aside from voices and Tate's and my footsteps was the ever-so-gentle lapping of the waves. It would have been disturbing if I hadn't been so confused and excited about what Tate had in mind.

Out on the deck, I saw Zeb and Ora lounging by the main mast, talking and smiling at each other in a distinctly conspiratorial manner. No other crew were in sight.

"Tate, what's, uh, what's happening?" I asked.

"It's a surprise," he said. He led me to Ora and Zeb. "We're just waiting on..."

Ezra emerged from below deck with a coil of rope slung over his shoulder and a piece of leather in his hand. I swallowed, my mouth going dry. I looked between all four of my lovers with wide eyes and a slowly dawning realisation.

They intended to what? Bind me and have their way with me on the deck, out in the open? In broad daylight?

Well, it was hardly broad daylight with all this confounded fog.

I looked around but the rest of the deck was empty.

"You can't be serious," I said, breathless. My cock was already straining against my trousers. Ora moved in behind me, slipped their hands around my waist and tugged my shirt open.

"You remember you can tell us to stop, right?" Ezra said. "But after a little discussion, we thought you might enjoy this..."

"Especially after what you said about us kidnapping you from the bedroom," Tate said.

I flushed with arousal and a certain amount of embarrassment, as Ora pulled me back against their chest and stroked their hands over my chest. They were so comforting, and their chest at my back grounded me enough that I could ask.

"What exactly *is* this, what do you have planned?"

"The rest of the crew are sleeping, after the watches, and have orders to stay below deck for the next hour or so," Tate said. "So that we can give you something."

"You've been so good, looking after all of us," Ora said, close to my ear.

"Calming us down," Tate added. He stepped closer and his hands went to the waistband of my trousers. My breath caught as his warm, rough fingers grazed my skin and he tugged the trousers open.

"Cheering us up," Ezra added. "We want to return the favour."

I swallowed, emotion welling in my throat and forming a sudden, embarrassing lump. "What? No, don't be ridiculous, you don't owe me anything!"

Ezra gently nudged Tate out of the way and fixed me with a stern look, stilling the rest of the protests I was going to make.

"We are going to pleasure you, pet, unless you tell us no. So." He lifted the dark brown leather collar that I had worn twice before, the little strip of leather that promised so much. "Yes, or no?"

I took a deep breath. Ora's hand had slipped down to my hip and my heart was beating fast.

I didn't feel like I deserved them all paying such attention to me, but did I *want* it? Absolutely, I wanted it.

"Yes," I said, nodding. I swallowed, feeling somewhat like I'd plunged into a lagoon with no idea how deep the water would be.

"Wonderful." Ezra nodded to Ora, who withdrew both their hands to pull my hair back and up, out of the way so that Ezra could slip the collar on my neck and fasten it tight.

Once that was done, Ora dropped my hair back and slipped their arms around my waist again.

Ezra gripped me by the back of the neck and kissed me hard, melting my knees so that I had to lean hard on Ora, breathless in an instant and my legs wobbly.

Ezra broke the kiss and suddenly Tate was there, slipping the rope off Ezra's shoulder and taking hold of one of my hands.

Zeb was suddenly on his knees - I hadn't even seen him move - pushing in between Ezra and I to strip my trousers off and lick at my cock with his curiously rough tongue. I gasped, trying to keep track of all the sensations I was feeling at once.

But that was impossible.

Ora's warm chest, covered with a thin layer of linen, pressed tight against my back, their hands caressing my stomach, my waist and chest. Teasing and comforting at the same time.

The tongue on my cock, making me hard and hot, Zeb on his knees, his eyes fixed on my face as I panted. His hand tugging my trousers to my ankles so I could step out of them.

Tate's hand pulling my arm out to the side, the roughness of rope looping my wrist and forearm and cinching tight as he knotted it. Sending a shiver through me for what it meant.

The tightness of the leather around my neck as I swallowed, close to feeling overwhelmed and uncertain of what was to happen next as my freedoms were taken away.

"Come on, Zeb, let us get him into position," Ezra said, putting a hand in Zeb's hair and tugging him gently back.

Zeb whined softly and I think I did too. "P-position?" I managed to ask.

Ora's hands on my hips and Tate tugging on the wrist he'd bound with rope guided me surely to the main mast.

I gazed up at the mast, and the rope on my wrist and

swallowed, starting to understand what was about to happen. My heart was pounding so hard it was almost all I could hear. I was afraid, out in the open like this, but at the same time, I trusted each of my lovers. I loved and trusted them, and that meant I trusted them to do what they said, to give me pleasure and to stop if I needed it.

I flushed with anticipation.

Oh Heaven, this is going to be a day to remember...

Ora turned me so my back was to the mast, and Tate passed the rope holding me behind it, and to Ezra, who took hold of my other hand.

Slowly, his eyes piercing mine, he kissed each of my fingertips and bit my thumb. I shivered and moaned, gazing at him with unbridled lust.

Then he tugged my arm back and looped rope around my other wrist, knotting it securely so I was bound to the mast of the ship. My hands couldn't quite touch each other when I strained, the mast was too wide for that, but it was solid at my back, which I was grateful for. Whatever happened next I wasn't confident I'd be able to stand for long unaided.

Tate produced the pot of oil from his waistcoat pocket and I swallowed, looking between them. Ora had their arms around Zeb now and the two of them were kissing, grinding against each other. I whined, aching to join them, to touch them, or more to the point, to be touched.

"Who's going first?" Ezra asked the others.

Tate eyed Ora and Zeb and shrugged. "I'll go first, if these two are so distracted." He stepped up to the mast, leaned in and kissed me, his hand on my jaw, cupping my face.

"Captain's privilege," Ezra chuckled.

"You look incredible like this," Tate murmured, kissing his

way along my jawline and to my neck. "I see what Ezra was talking about with the collar. It's gorgeous. You two will have to allow me along to your next little... training session."

"God, yes," I breathed. The idea of Tate seeing me in the leather harness. Or better, the image I kept returning to of Tate, bound and helpless under me... I was already hard and aching, even more stimulation almost felt cruel, even if it was just mental.

"Mm," Tate tugged gently on the collar and I gasped, finding his mouth and kissing it harder, aware of the ache of my need.

"Please, Tate, please touch me." I gasped against his cheek when he stopped kissing me.

"With pleasure." Tate slipped a hand below my rear and lifted me clear off the ground. The wood of the mast rough against my back, and the ropes on my wrists tugging in a delicious way with the change of position.

I moaned as his finger, now slick with oil, found my ass and started to tease me open. I wished then, that whatever magic I might possibly possess could work like Ora's and allow me to stretch and slick myself naturally. It would make this process a lot less arduous, although arduous was hardly the correct word... my mind was spinning with desire.

My body demanding something that I couldn't take for myself.

Exquisite torture.

I wrapped my legs around Tate's waist and locked my ankles together, tipped my head back against the mast and moaned loud enough that the others would hear me.

"That's it, that's a good boy," Ezra's rough growl, from a few steps away. I dropped my chin and searched him out. He had one hand on Zeb's waist, caressing him there, his other hand slowly stroking his own cock.

My body jolted with more arousal.

Ora had lost their clothes on the deck and was working to undress Zeb, sinking to their knees.

"Please Tate," I gasped. "Please, I need to feel you inside me, I need more, please."

"Of course, love," Tate said. "You're going to come so much today, so many times. Anything you want, you can have it. Though, the sound of you begging for it is definitely working for me."

He shifted, and I felt the warm, velvet head of him pressing against me. He pushed slowly inside and the both of us moaned with the hot, sliding drag of it.

My arms twitched, wanting to lace themselves around his neck but finding only the ropes binding me. That sent another thrill of desire through me.

"Nothing you have to do but take it," Tate murmured. His mouth found my neck again, biting at the skin above the collar, then at the collar itself. I jolted against him, trying to thrash but with nowhere to go, no movement in my arms.

"Stars," I breathed. "How will I survive this?"

Tate chuckled and his hand came up to stroke my hair, a tender, kind gesture, considering.

"You will," he said. "You're strong, you're amazing, Gideon. I love you so much."

I closed my eyes, pressing my head against his as he started to thrust into me. Each movement filled me and made me moan louder still.

"Best not drag this out too much, though," he said. And with that he sped up his pace. I was bouncing in his arms, the sturdy mast helping to balance us as he thrusted into me.

Behind Tate I could hear more sounds of pleasure, so I opened my eyes to see Ora bobbing their head on Zeb's cock as Ezra ground against his rear, the three of them making a tableaux so arousing that I almost came then.

"Oh Christ, oh sweet Lord above," I said.

"Come on, Gideon," Tate said. He reached between us and finally, *finally*, fisted my aching cock. "Let me feel it, let them hear it, show us how good it feels."

I didn't need any more encouragement. My orgasm crashed through my body like a huge wave, every muscle tensed and then released and I felt my cock pumping hot liquid over Tate's hand and my stomach. I cried out, something that could have been Tate's name, but was mostly wordless.

In an instant, Tate was coming too, shoving up inside me with something like a roar and shuddering with the force of it. I felt him fill me and something in me shifted, any lingering trace of nervousness and uncertainty evaporated entirely.

I felt liberated somehow. Freed of any kind of judgement or fear, and flooded with joy.

Tate pressed his forehead to mine, trapping my head pleasantly against the mast. I was panting hard, and so was he. "Well, fuck," he said, finally. "Why didn't we think of this earlier?"

I laughed then, almost from surprise rather than mirth, although the idea was heady and amusing. "I'm sure I don't know," I managed to reply. Tate laughed harder and shook his head at me, his eyes crinkling with affection and something almost like awe.

"You're amazing, Gideon."

He eased out of me and I uncrossed my ankles, letting my legs drop down as he lowered me to my feet.

He kissed me again, fervently, as if he could never get enough of me, and I kissed him back just as hard, knowing that I'd never tire of this man. That I could definitely never have my fill of him.

Finally, he broke the kiss and half turned to the others. "If you're all too busy, then I'll just continue to keep Gideon entertained," he said. "Happy to take care of him."

"Uh uh," Ora said. They wiped their mouth and went to stand up. "I'll go."

"Me first," Zeb said, peeling themselves away from Ezra. "You've all had more time with Gideon than I have, in human form anyway. In this form where we get to mate."

I flushed, pleased and a little embarrassed that they'd squabble over me like that.

"Fine," Ora said, and stroked a hand down Ezra's chest, tugging his shirt open. Tate moved back, beside Ezra, and slipped an arm around his waist. Ezra seemed to prickle at the sudden attention from both of them, but relaxed when he saw me watching. He shot me a wink, and turned to kiss Tate hard on the mouth.

I moaned, watching them, until Zeb cleared his throat.

"Pay attention to me," he ordered. I looked at him instantly, heat pooling in my stomach at the order, and the reminder that I was tied up, and Zeb was not.

He moved closer, not touching me but only by the tiniest distance. I sucked a breath in, looking him in the eyes. It was almost hypnotic, the way he looked at me. My every nerve felt taut and fully at attention.

Suddenly, Zeb didn't seem at all like a small, cute kitty cat.

He appeared more like a lion, or a jaguar, the top of the food chain. Looking at me like I was his dinner.

Trapped as I was, I started panting again, straining towards him, because even though there was something frightening in it, I wanted him so intensely.

"Gideon," he breathed, his voice barely audible. This close I could see the traces of grey in the hair at his temples. The shininess of the scars across his nose and over his left eye. The subtle texture of his skin.

"Zebulon," I said. Full name seemed appropriate for some reason. Maybe because it felt more... respectful?

Without warning he pressed himself against me, his hands moving over my sides, running down my arms where they were bound behind me, then up to caress my neck and my jaw.

I'd never seen him like this, so intense, so in control. So... Mesmerising.

He ground against me, our cocks sliding together and making me whine. I hadn't thought, after the intensity of my orgasm with Tate, that I'd be ready quite so soon, but my body was more than willing to cooperate with my lovers' plans.

"I'm going to fuck you, and then suck you off," he murmured. "You'd better not come before my mouth is on you."

My jaw worked and I tried to protest. "I-, uh, I don't think I can hold it back... like that, please, Zeb."

"You will."

He pushed into me, slick and easy from Tate's stretching me, I was soaking back there from the oil and from Tate's seed. It was also very sensitive from Tate's ministrations and it made Zeb's cock feel even more incredible.

The noise I made was a high pitched one, a kind of cry mixed with a gasp, tearing from the back of my throat.

196

Zeb started to rumble, a purr unlike his happy contented one, more like the purr of a beast who has caught the thing he was chasing and now intended to enjoy it.

His strong, muscular arm curled around my waist and he shoved into me. All this time his eyes never left mine, and I hardly dared to blink. I felt utterly transfixed, pushing up on my toes to allow him more access to me.

His free hand reached for my left thigh and hoisted it up, bending my leg so I had the flat of my left foot braced on the mast, my knee splayed out to the side. He shoved in, far deeper than before and I whimpered, almost sobbing from the glorious sensation of being utterly used.

I'm not allowed to come. I thought, and I bit down hard on my lip. *Mustn't let it happen. I don't want to know what happens if Zeb is displeased... his punishment might be intense. Don't think about how good it feels.*

Don't think.

But that was impossible. Every time he bucked his hips I responded with a cry or a moan. His arm pulled me closer, taut against his stomach and he finally broke eye contact with me to close his eyes and groan. His hips moved far faster now, pumping into me with a furious, pounding rhythm.

I let my head fall forward, bracing my mouth on his shoulder, kissing him as I moaned. Through half closed eyes I saw Ezra watching. His eyes were full of lust, never stilling as he looked over Zeb and me.

In fact, all three of them seemed to be watching as I blinked and gasped, my mouth leaving wet marks on Zeb's shoulder, Tate had his arm around Ezra, curled up to stroke at his chest.

Ora leaned against Ezra on the other side, their hand down his trousers, but moving almost lazily.

Getting him ready for me? The thought almost made me come on the spot, well... that and Zeb's back arching, his cock slamming deep inside me and his yowling howl of pleasure as he filled me with his seed.

I clenched my eyes shut and bit down on his shoulder, willing my body not to follow suit. Behind the mast my hands fisted, my toes curled into the deck and the mast, so much of me *wanting completion* so hard, but a larger part wanting more to please.

I wanted to play the game properly, and my part was to do what I was told. I wanted to please Zeb, for him to be proud of me, and that meant denying my body what it wanted.

Zeb was breathing heavily against my ear.

"Good." He growled as he pulled out of me without art, making me gasp and have to clench down on my desires again. I bit him again, because it had seemed to help last time, and he hummed his approval. When I had control of myself, I straightened my head up and licked my lips - was that blood?

How hard had I bitten him?

Zeb didn't seem concerned about my teeth marks in his shoulder. He tapped my left leg and I put my foot back on the deck, shifting both feet a couple of times and leaning against the mast a bit more.

I tried to breathe deeper, to regain composure, but it was utterly impossible. I was wrecked. A panting, needing mess.

Thankfully Zeb wasted no time in going to his knees and closing his mouth around my cock.

"Oh, Lord, oh stars," the words fell out of my mouth without bypassing my brain. "Oh please, good lord, please Zeb, *fuck*..." Every curse and plea I knew was pouring out of me.

He took me deep into his throat, sucking and licking and soon my body was acting on its own - twitching and tensing.

"I'm going to..." I managed to gasp, and then went back to cursing.

Zeb's hand found my balls and he rubbed them between his thumb and forefinger.

I couldn't hold back any more. I tossed my head side to side as my body let go of what I'd held back. Like a dam breaking it washed over me, shuddering with the sheer satisfaction of release.

Zeb swallowed around me, taking everything I had to give and then licking me clean thoroughly with his quick, pink tongue.

When he moved back, my knees gave way and I crumpled to the deck, my top half kept upright only by the ropes holding me to the mast.

Zeb moved back in on his knees, rubbed his cheek against mine and pressed a hand to my chest.

"You did so well, Gideon," he rumbled.

His purr seemed to loan a growl to his voice. It was something resonant and utterly beautiful, and distinct from the gravel filled growl Ezra used. "I'm proud of you, you're very brave, very strong. You're so full of love, Gideon..."

I was panting and weak, trembling from the exertions, but his praise of me filled something in my heart. It felt as if it warmed the pit of my soul, and I felt so grateful.

So thankful to the universe, to God above, to the men around me... That I could have this, that my lovers would want to give me this, to make me the centre of everything for a time.

I felt tears spring to my eyes. Bliss, release, love, gratitude, it was fast overwhelming me. I knew I was flushed and smiling like a fool. Zeb pressed his cheek against me and purred, still praising me, lending me some of his strength, some of his steadiness.

I can't believe I have two more lovers to go, and then I don't know what is planned. I'm the luckiest man on Earth.

CHAPTER TWENTY - IN WHICH GIDEON GETS A SLIGHT REPRIEVE BEFORE CONTINUING

*A*fter a couple of minutes I had better control of my emotions and I sat back on my heels, although with my arms still bound it was somewhat awkward.

Zeb moved more upright, stroking my hair and still telling me lovely things, bolstering me up.

"You're the best boy in the world, the bravest and strongest..." he murmured.

"Drink?" Tate asked, and I blinked up at him, wondering when he'd had the time to retrieve the jug and cup I saw in his hands.

I nodded, and he pressed the cup to my lips, and I drank gratefully.

The water was cool, and I took three greedy swallows before Tate took the cup back. "More?"

I cleared my throat - it still felt rough and raw from moaning, my mouth slightly dry.

"Yes, please, Tate." He helped me sip more water.

Zeb shifted to beside me, laying his head on my shoulder and holding me with a hand around my waist.

Ezra and Ora watched, Ezra with undisguised lust, with *wanting*, and Ora with a kind of approving smile.

My memory stirred... although I was largely afraid of the world under the sea, when we'd first met Ora had said that mating down there was very free. Maybe this kind of thing was something they'd participated in before?

Ezra... I felt that Ezra certainly had done things like this previously. Probably hosted wild parties in Tortuga with that girl, and who knows who else? The people from the leather works?

"How are you holding up?" Tate asked, crouching beside me. He smoothed some hair back from my forehead.

I tore my eyes from Ezra and Ora and smiled at him instead. His eyebrows were drawn together, and I saw I needed to reassure him.

"Wonderful," I said, it came out like a dreamy sigh.

Tate's eyes crinkled and his teeth flashed. He kissed my cheek. "Enjoying yourself then? Good surprise?"

"The best," I said. "Yes, this is... Honestly, this is more than I deserve."

Tate shook his head. "I disagree, and this lot do too. You're special, Gideon, and we want to show you how special you are to us."

He pushed his fingers through my hair, pulling it back and I leaned my head against his hand. Zeb chuckled, nuzzling me on the other side. I flushed with happiness, feeling my heart swell again and tears prickling, tears of pure joy.

Ora pulled away from Ezra and ambled over.

"All right, it's my turn," they said, giving me a suggestive smile and raising an eyebrow. I shivered as Zeb kissed my cheek and unfolded himself, standing up and stretching, arching his back and sauntering towards Ezra.

So Ezra was last, that figured. He was the kind of man who always wanted the last word...

I shifted, trying to get my feet under me so I could stand again but Ora held up a hand and I stopped moving.

"Stay down there," Ora said. "I have an idea, something a little different..."

I looked up at them, swallowing in anticipation. Ora was always fun, and looking up at them from my position, bound and fucked open as I was, my body hypersensitive from the previous two lovers, I felt ready for anything.

I thought I'd better say that out loud so they knew.

"Anything you like," I said, licking my lips.

Ora moved closer, lining their cock up to my mouth and I groaned happily, leaning my head forward to lick at them.

I was greedy for the hot, salt taste of them and my tongue moved quickly. I rolled my eyes up to watch their face, and saw Ora had braced a hand on the mast, their head dropped forward to watch me work. Their eyes large, pupils blown black and wide with pleasure.

God above, is it possible to die from happiness?

I pushed my head down on their cock, determined to replicate what Zeb had done for me, gagging as their cock hit the back of my throat.

I pulled back and tried again, pushing my tongue up against the underside of their shaft, caressing the veiny thickness of it.

Ora was panting now, continuing to watch me, one hand in my hair, tugging and fisting it as I worked.

"That's it, Gid, just like that, feels so good, you're doing so well." I moaned and repeated the movement, breathing hard through my nose, moving faster as I felt Ora's cock pulsing on my tongue.

Soon they were bucking into my mouth and I closed my eyes and took it, pushing my feet against the deck and moaning, hands fisting again, tugging at the ropes just to feel them cut into my skin.

Ora cried out and pulled back abruptly. I'd barely had time to lick my lips before they were seated in my lap, pushing themselves down on top of my swollen cock.

"Oh Ora," I rasped, unable to say much more than that.

"You don't have to say anything," Ora said. "Just enjoy it, my darling."

Ora hitched their knees up beside my chest, wiggled side to side to shove themselves further down onto me, and then leaned their torso back, laying almost horizontal on my outstretched legs, only their hips staying marginally upright.

I took a deep breath and it came out of me in a bodily shudder.

Ora has given me no orders except to enjoy it, and they called me darling.

And now they're laying down as if putting on a show for the others.

I leaned back against the mast, resting my head and rolled my hips slowly up into them. Ora moaned, writhing on top of me, expression one of complete, consuming bliss.

Tate and Zeb were touching each other, Zeb's hand tugging on Tate slowly as Tate stroked Zeb's chest. Both sets of eyes were fixed on Ora and myself.

Ezra stood a little back from the others now, arms folded,

eyes sparkling with promise. But I couldn't think of that now. Instead I closed my eyes and focused entirely on what I was feeling.

My cock, buried inside Ora, who writhed and dipped like the sea itself, wave after wave of new sensations, all of them wonderful.

The tightness in my chest from trying to catch my breath, my heart pounding as another orgasm built inside me. The chafe and tug on my wrists, bound with rope and trapped behind me, adding its own forbidden, almost painful stimulation. My fucked open hole, smarting a little, the best kind of ache. The knowledge that whatever my lovers were going to do with me, helpless as I was, that it would be endlessly enjoyable, gratifying even. To give and receive like this, and to trust them with so much, it was so rewarding.

"Ora," I breathed, their name like a prayer on my tongue. "Ora, Ora..."

Ora sat up then, nimble and limber, and kissed me passionately, our tongues twining and lapping at each other with alacrity.

Ora's hips never stopped their rock and pull, the intoxicating surge of my own hips moving almost on their own.

"Come with me, Gideon, Gideon darling, I love you so much," Ora murmured into my mouth. I kissed their lips by way of answer and they wound their arms around me and pressed tight against me.

Without another word, our bodies moved and we came in the same instant, my eyes snapped shut in the moment, but I seemed to see the ocean itself as if I were under it.

Light filtered down in shafts from above. Currents tugged me this way and that, but I wasn't afraid. I knew I was safe here, I was with Ora, fucking Ora, but somehow I was under the sea as well, watching fish swim and seaweed float past.

After a few long moments I opened my eyes. Ora had stopped moving and was pressing their forehead to mine, breathing in time with me.

"What was that?" I asked, barely above the sound of a breath.

"I don't know," Ora said, at the same volume. "But I think it was your magic... I've never... That's not happened to me before."

I smiled, flooded with joy, and kissed them again. I didn't know what this magic was, but if it gave me more of a connection to Ora, or to any of my lovers, then I knew it had to be a good thing, not an evil one.

"I love you so much," I said, a little louder.

"I love you, Gideon." They kissed me again and then smiled, breaking the spell - whatever it was - between us and standing up. "Are you ready for Ezra?"

I was feeling giddy, my head still drifting under the ocean, my body stuffed with happiness and stimulation. Maybe I was over stimulated? Was that a thing that could happen?

"Lord, no," I said, laughing. "Is anyone ever ready for Ezra?"

"I heard that," Ezra said.

He kissed Ora on the mouth and I'm sure I heard him say "good work" to them before he moved in front of me, barely past the reach of my toes. He folded his arms, examining me. I looked up at him, smiling so wide it felt it was stretching my cheeks.

"Look at you," he said, and I swear there was affection under the rough growl of his voice. My heart thumped happily.

"Fucked out, blissed out, orgasm-drunk... You're a mess, pet."

I squirmed, happy and unfazed by his words, bold with it all. "I'm sure you would be too, in my position," I said.

"Mmm," he said. "Perhaps. But we're talking about you, and you're still wearing my collar, remember?"

I swallowed, something sounding in the back of my head, a warning signal. But it was too late now.

"Should I stand up? I may need some assistance," I said, suppressing a giggle.

Ezra licked his lips and nodded. "Yes, stand up." He moved around behind the mast and loosened the ropes from my wrists. This was unexpected, but welcome. The muscles in my arms seemed to groan as I rolled my shoulders and stretched my arms in front of me.

"Stand up," Ezra said. He moved back in front of me and coiled the rope. I swallowed, rubbing my wrist with one hand before planting both hands on the deck and pushing up into a standing position.

My legs felt a little wobbly, a little stiff. I combed my hands through my hair, which was somewhat tangled by now, my hands trembled a little.

"Like this?" I asked, tipping my chin up to look at Ezra, smiling at him, fluttering my eyelashes. He moved in close to me and hissed.

"I want to show the others what a good pet you are, and you're choosing *now* to be disobedient?"

Oh, ohhh...

I swallowed again and dropped my hands to my side, straightened my spine and cleared my throat.

"I'm sorry, Sir," I said, quietly. The bubbly, excited feeling was still there underneath, but I focused on staying still and listening in case Ezra had any orders for me.

"You will be," Ezra said. "Give me your wrists."

I watched his face, lifting my hands in between us and pressing them together, as if I was praying. "Like this?"

"Call me Sir," he grunted.

"Sir."

"If you think I'm going easy on you just because you've already been had by three other people, you're incorrect."

I shivered and my skin flashed hot at those words. "Yes, Sir," I said. "I understand, I'll behave, Sir. I want to make you look good."

He wound the ropes around my wrists several times over, looping and knotting it double width of the previous ropes, and strangely comfortable because of it. When Ezra was done knotting it, there was a long dangling piece hanging loose. This he took in his hand and yanked, forcing my arms up and over my head.

"Stay still," he commanded. I nodded and concentrated on maintaining the position, focusing on my breathing and keeping it steady.

He threw the rope up over the spar and caught the end when it came down on the other side, then secured the end so that the rope was taut, holding my arms up and utterly trapping me.

"What happens to disobedient pets?" He asked, loud enough that the others could hear.

Oh God, he was taking a page from Ora's book and making it a show. Lord preserve me.

"I uh," I stuttered, my mind racing. I had to answer his question. "Uh, punishment, Sir."

"That's right. How do you feel about the whip?"

The whip? How did I feel about the whip? Afraid? Most people were afraid of the whip. But then... this was Ezra. If he was suggesting it, it wouldn't be a pure punishment. This wasn't the same as a punishment in the Navy.

I swallowed, struggled to answer. "I uh, Sir, I don't... I- I don't know. But I trust you, Sir."

That seemed like a good answer to me, at least.

"Good boy," Ezra said. He finally smiled, kissing me so thoroughly, so forcefully that I likely would have crumpled to the deck again if the ropes hadn't been suspending me up right. It felt as if my bones had melted, in the best possible way.

"Just a lash or two, to see how you like it," he said, when he pulled back. His voice cracked a little and I realised that in all this time, he mustn't have come himself.

He'd been teased, grinding on the others, stroked and God knows what else, but he'd saved himself for me.

I was flattered - and a little afraid.

Ezra stalked past Tate and produced the whip from somewhere. Tate, Ora and Zeb had all sat down on the deck, leaning against the benches to watch as if what was about to happen were a show put on for their entertainment.

And actually, it is.

"Sorry pet, but you'll face the mast for this one. Brace yourself if you can."

Ezra gripped me by the hips and turned me. I spread my legs apart for a more sturdy stance, leaned my arms on the mast as best I could and pressed my forehead against my arms. Ezra hadn't left me a lot of slack in the ropes, but this I could manage.

"Ready?" Ezra asked, pressing a kiss between my shoulder blades in the spot he always seemed to find.

Every other time he's done something that hurts, my body has turned it into sweet pleasure. There's no reason this would be any different.

"Yes, Sir."

All the same, I flinched with the crack of the whip, and when it licked its stinging lash against my back I cried out.

The pain was unbelievable, a white hot stinging pain, and I jolted, knocking my head hard against my arms. But as soon as the heat of it cooled, my body flushed with enjoyment.

The sting sent sparks throughout my body, shooting through my spine up to my head, up my arms, and down my legs, then pouring into my groin to make my cock swell all over again.

"How was it, pet?" Ezra asked. He was close in behind me now, I hadn't heard him move. Hadn't heard anything in fact, I'd been so focused on what my body was doing with the sensations.

"More," I gasped, then licked my lips. "Please Sir, it's so good, I want more. Please!"

Ezra gripped my hair, turned my head and kissed me hard enough I tasted blood then turned to the others. "He asked for more!"

I heard Tate, Ora and Zeb all cheer and shout words of encouragement, but they all seemed distant to me.

My lip had split, it stung when I licked it again, and the taste of blood on my tongue was almost another pleasure on top of all the others.

There was another crack and I felt the lash of the whip once more. This time my body knew what to do, and the process of pain into warmth and arousal was far more swift.

"Yes, yes," I moaned, wanting Ezra to know I liked it, that he could - and should - continue.

I'm not sure how many times Ezra lashed me, as I seemed to lose sense of things like numbers, or sounds.

I couldn't hear anything beyond the crack of the whip and my own ragged breathing. Everything in me focused on the sting on my back, which grew with each blow, and the increasing ache in my cock. I needed to come, but to do that, I'd need Ezra's permission.

Finally, the lashing stopped and Ezra's hand clamped around my waist. "Still with us, pet?"

I pressed back against him then hissed as my tender back met his chest, flinching forward again even as I moaned.

"B-barely," I said. Then, "Sir."

"It's all right," he said, and gently nibbled my ear. "You did well, you made me so proud, pet."

I smiled and relaxed my shoulders, Ezra was happy with me. That was all I needed... Well, that and just one other thing.

"Want to make you happy," I murmured. I opened my eyes but it felt like such an effort.

"You do," Ezra said. His fingers probed at me, teasing at the fucked open hole and slipping more oil in before he pushed in himself. He was being surprisingly gentle with me, or possibly, everything felt gentle after the whip.

His arm around me shifted and he braced my chest with his hand, holding me steady as he rocked his hips. "That's it, that's a good boy," he murmured, kissing my neck and shoulder. "You took so much and now you're taking this too. You're so good, so brave, and so strong."

His other hand started to pump my cock and I gasped. It was unbelievable to think I still had more to give but apparently I did. My body was surging with fire, sparks of hot desire shooting from the parts of my back Ezra was touching. From his lips, from his hands.

I was so safe, so well cared for, so *cherished*. That was the feeling. Ezra was cherishing me, they all were.

I closed my eyes and surrendered completely to him.

"Come when you need to, pet," Ezra said. And I nodded, feeling less urgency now, just love and a serene sensation of belonging.

Belonging to Ezra. belonging on this ship. Belonging to all of my lovers, and not one more than the other, but to all equally, and knowing that they belonged to me in turn.

I felt so much love it felt like it was radiating out of me in beams of light. As if I was some kind of sun.

Ezra was panting in my ear, getting close, and I squeezed down on him consciously, uncertain how I was doing it but that it felt as natural as breathing.

We reached completion in the same moment, the way Ora and I had. Something within me instinctively feeling when it was time to release.

After all the orgasms I'd already had, this one was less Earth-shattering and more... natural. Something about it just felt right, so entirely perfect that it made me feel complete. Which wasn't to say it wasn't intense, I was shouting, almost screaming with the pressure of the relief, the noise tearing out of my throat.

Ezra grunted and groaned, loud in my ear.

I slumped forward as much as I was able to, panting hard.

"All right?" Ezra asked, finally, kissing my shoulder as his hips came to a rest.

I nodded, words were still a little beyond me.

"Right then, now, let's see if we want to continue the party out here, or take it to the cabin, eh?"

Continue? Oh good Lord, I really am going to pass out...

But the idea was wonderful as well, of course I wanted to continue, to be able to touch and kiss my lovers when I wished to.

Ezra pulled out of me with a grunt and turned to the others, his arm still around my waist, half supporting me.

I heard something, faintly, a bell perhaps? Maybe I was imagining it.

"Well, lads?" Ezra called out. "What's next?"

"Zeb, what is it?"

"Smell something." Was that Zeb? I heard the sound of footsteps.

Then a shout in a voice I didn't recognise.

"There they are!"

A curious whirring noise, and a thump, followed by several more. Ezra let go of me and swore, I slumped against the mast, half turning to see what was happening. My eyes were bleary and I didn't understand right away.

Grappling hooks dug into the deck.

Ezra reaching for a sword that wasn't at his hip.

Tate scrambling, naked, towards the nearest weapon.

Shouts and raised weapons and men pouring over the side of the Grey Kelpie, they were dressed in the blues of the Royal Navy.

Ora blinked in confusion and then hurried forward, teeth bared.

Zeb took a blow to the jaw, hissed and slashed a clawed hand at the man's face.

A deep, shuddering thump and the ship deck rocking hard

under my feet. I crashed into the mast, pain jolting through my jaw as I tried to keep my feet.

My blood ran cold as my mind processed the impossible scene in front of me. All the bliss and serenity I'd been feeling evaporated into bone shaking shock.

We were being boarded.

CHAPTER TWENTY-ONE - IN WHICH GIDEON IS RESCUED

"*N*o, confound it, stop!" I shouted, tugging uselessly against the rope holding me. Ezra was too good at his craft by half. There was no give in the knots and I was trapped, naked and exposed against the mast as the Naval officers quickly overpowered my lovers.

They'd been caught off guard, naked, unarmed.

No reason to assume any danger, after all the fog was still thick as pea soup.

How had they found us? How had they come here? And why now?

An ordinary officer approached me and using his sabre, cut the rope above my head. He carefully averted his eyes from my nakedness, although his face blazed red.

"There now, Master Keene, you're safe now," he said, stiffly. It felt good to have my arms down from above me but the knots still held and I couldn't get the ropes off my wrists.

"Ah," he said, and expertly slipped the blade of his weapon under the biggest knot. The ropes fell away. He shrugged off his coat and slipped it over my shoulders.

"I don't care about that," I said.

Where was Tate? I looked over to see him with his hands up, three men's sabres pointed at his throat.

Ezra was flat on his front, two men working to restrain him. His shearwater tattoo clear and exposed to the men.

Zeb was on the ground as well, guarded by another man. Ora was cornered, hissing and baring their teeth at a troupe of five.

My heart ached, panic making my breath rasp from my mouth. The enemy didn't seem to be striking any killing blows, which was something, at least.

"Please," I said to the man beside me. "You've got the wrong ship, this isn't..."

"You're Gideon Keene, aren't you? You match the description," he said.

I pulled the coat around myself, winced as the rough fabric hit the tender, whipped skin of my back and then winced again as I saw the enemy advancing on Ora. They were backed against the railing of the ship, but that was hardly a trap for the merfolk.

"Ora! Go overboard! Save yourself!" I cried.

Ora's eyes flicked up to me, and then to the others, and back to the sabres. "Please, Ora!" I shouted.

Ora neatly flipped backwards off the ship and there was a soft splash.

The men who had been menacing them looked confused, rushed to the side and looked overboard.

I couldn't breathe, my chest was too tight.

Chains were being brought over from the British ship.

Tate was forced to his knees.

My head felt too hot, too light.

Ezra was clapped in irons, his eyes on me, full of anger and fear.

"I can't..." I breathed. The man beside me took me by my elbow.

"Here comes the captain."

Then a man stepped over onto the deck of the Kelpie. My knees went out from under me. It was Captain Thornton... the man I'd served under in my ill-fated year in the Navy. My mind went dark and I blacked out.

When I woke up it was in an unfamiliar room.

This is happening to me far too often. I thought. *Ever since I left home.*

My wrists felt strange, heavy, and I lifted one to see it was wadded in gauze and bandages. Both of them were.

There was something under my rear as well, some kind of cushion or bandaging there. Over my back as well, now that I was taking stock of things. I was dressed in loose linen underclothes and a wool blanket was draped over me.

I looked around. I was in a narrow cot in a ship's cabin. The skeleton sketches and herbal diagrams, along with the smell of astringent told me it was an infirmary, and there was no one else in the room.

I wasn't restrained at all, but when I sat up my head swam unpleasantly and my stomach lurched. If there'd been any food in there I might have been sick, but I hadn't eaten at all that day. I groaned in pain.

Wait, how long was I asleep? Was it still the same day? Oh Lord, what's happened to my lovers?

The door to the room opened and my breath caught.

A short ensign in long blue pants and a white shirt entered the room, startled when he saw me sitting up and then sighed, trying to calm himself. One hand on his chest.

"Right, you're awake then. How's the pain?"

"Uh, no pain, not really," I said. "What's going on?"

"You were kidnapped by pirates," he said, his eyes going wide. "They were doing all sorts of unspeakable things to you. It's probably best if you don't remember."

"I wasn't, they weren't," I said, shortly. "I'm not kidnapped, well, I might be now. I meant what's happening now, what ship is this? Where are we bound?"

He eyed me uncertainly and set down a pile of folded clothing.

"We're on the HMS Trinity Royal," he said. "Captain Thornton would like to speak with you when you feel strong enough."

My stomach sank. I had managed to put out of my mind that the Captain was my old Captain. There was a man who truly knew how useless I had been in my year of service.

But I had to know what had happened. I rubbed my forehead with the palm of my hand, willing my head to stop aching.

"Before that, can you catch me up, please?" I asked. "Ensign, uh...?" I raised and eyebrow.

"Jacobs," he said. "Zacharias Jacobs. But you can call me Zack."

"Pleased to meet you, I'm Gideon," I said, almost without thinking.

Stupid preparatory school manners. I sounded like we were in a garden party being introduced, not in a crisis situation where I've been kidnapped by the Royal Fleet.

"I know. You're Gideon Keene. We're headed back to Kingston now to return you to your father," Zack said.

I groaned and rubbed my entire face. My stomach roiled again and I swallowed the urge to vomit. "No, why?"

"Why, because you were kidnapped, of course. And Captain Thornton says we're to be showered with riches, especially since we captured those pirates too."

My heart thumped dully. At least he'd said captured and not hanged. The idea of Tate, Ezra and the others being hanged while I slept in an infirmary almost made me throw up again.

"Which pirates are those?" My throat was scratchy and hoarse. Zack poured me a cup of water and handed it to me, I sipped it gratefully. I eyed him. He seemed an all right sort. He hadn't called me any names for being found naked, bound and fucked out. He seemed excited about the money but I got a feeling of kindness from him.

"Only the Shearwater pirate and Tate the Bloody," Zack said. He rolled his eyes expressively. "Didn't you even know who you was kidnapped by?"

"I wasn't kidnapped, I ran away," I said, gritting my teeth.

"Hmm," Zack said. "Anyway, a message's been sent to the Governor, and we should have you back home with him within a fortnight."

"How did... How did you even find the ship?" I asked. "The fog was so thick and there was no wind, no one should have been sailing in conditions like that."

At that Zack shivered and traced the sign of the cross over their body. "I can't say, Master Keene."

"Please just call me Gideon," I said.

"I don't understand it myself, except it was awful strange. The Captain said he had strange dreams..." he stopped short and cleared his throat. "It doesn't matter. You're safe now, is the important thing."

Strange dreams. Could it be Solomon? Could Solomon have summoned up a fog to stop us and lead the Royal Navy straight to us? Is that... How would that benefit him?

Tate will be hanged in Kingston. Solomon... I got the feeling Solomon wanted to kill him himself. Or just... Keep him, somehow?

"The pirates you mentioned..." I picked up the folded shirt and pulled it on, it was the perfect size. The bandages over my back meant the welts from the whipping didn't do much more than throb gently when the shirt came down over them. "Where are they being kept?"

"Well, most of the crew is in the brig of the Kelpie," Zack said. "But the really valuable ones, the Shearwater and Bloody Tate, they're in the brig on the Trinity. Kept under constant guard, shackled and all. Bloody exciting if you ask me."

He leaned in, smiling as if to share in a joke but I looked away, chewing on my lip. Zack cleared his throat and took a step back towards the door.

"Well, if you're feeling all right, let's get you to the Captain. Then we can find you a meal."

My stomach rumbled, even though the last thing I wanted to do was eat. I pulled on the simple blue trousers, twins to the ones Zack wore. Then I reached inside and tore the bandaging off my rear. It had felt like wearing a napkin. Zack raised his eyebrows and looked away, cheeks flushing.

Interesting reaction.

But this is not the time to dwell on Zack.

This whole situation is utterly terrible, Tate and Ezra chained in the brig, Ora somewhere in the ocean, Zeb... Who knows where? The crew of the Kelpie, Sagorika, Anton, Shem... all locked up and it's all my fault.

I have to make this right, somehow.

"Right," I said, trying to summon up some courage. My head was throbbing still, and my legs felt stiff and weak under me. But there was nothing else to be done. "Take me to the Captain, if you please."

.... *To be continued.*

Keep a weather eye out for His Piratical Harem book three:
Merfolk's Soulmate

If you enjoyed this book, please consider leaving a review on Amazon. Indie authors rely on star ratings and reviews to go up the algorithm and be seen by more readers.

Sign up for my newsletter for updates on new releases
https://www.subscribepage.com/q4c4no
Come join Drake's Crew reader's group to meet other fans and get exclusive content – maybe
you'll even get to name a character in the next book
https://www.facebook.com/groups/1272511269588779/

Come and visit Drake online:
Twitter: https://twitter.com/DrakeLamarque
Pinterest: https://www.pinterest.nz/drakelamarque/
Newsletter: https://www.subscribepage.com/q4c4no

Thanks to everyone who bought Cabin Boy, and to everyone who reviewed it. This series was a gamble, a calculated risk, and I'm so glad it's paid off and people have enjoyed the adventures of Gideon and his frankly ridiculous number of lovers.

I'm loving writing this series, and it wouldn't be possible without the support of my gorgeous, fantastic, Tate-esque partner for life Yuki. Thanks for everything, Prince Fucking Charming. And I'm so sorry about this cliffhanger.

Thanks also to my magical beta-reader. Without your love for the characters, your eye for continuity - not to mention body positions in the sex scenes - and your brilliant suggestions this book wouldn't be half what it is.

BOOK ONE OF HIS PIRATICAL HAREM – CABIN BOY

Buy Now

I've never been what I was supposed to be. Wealthy sons of Port Governors aren't supposed to be ejected from the British Navy after less than a year, they're not supposed to like pulp romances or daydream about the handsome heroes of the stories instead of the heroines.

When my Father issued me an order to marry a woman, I knew I had no choice but to make my own way in the world, and I found a berth on the first ship out of Jamaica.

I didn't mean to join a pirate ship, and I certainly didn't intend to find myself the cabin boy to an incredibly charming Pirate Captain. Or that I'd also be attracted to the mysterious First Mate, or that both of them would show me all sorts of unspeakable and salacious pleasures while on board. How can I choose just one of them when I want both?

In addition to confusion on board the ship, there's also enchanting gender fluid merfolk, a cat which seems to understand a lot more than it should, an unseasonable storm and a sea witch with a serious grudge... and with all these complications, I am definitely in over my head.

Come and meet the crew:

Gideon: an innocent with a lot of forbidden desires and a lot of love to give

Tate: a huge, muscular ship's captain with a sweet side

Ezra: a dominant and closed off first mate

Ora: a genderqueer, curious and affectionate merfolk

ALSO PUBLISHED BY GREY KELPIE STUDIO

Rival Princes by Jaxon Knight

There are three golden rules for new recruits at Fairyland Theme Park:

1. No breaking character, even if you're dying of heat exhaustion
    2. Always give guests the most magical time
    3. No falling in love.

Nate's only been at work one day, and he's already broken all three.

Fast-tracked into a Prince role, Nate's at odds with Dash, the handsome not-so-charming prince who is supposed to be training him. Nate doesn't know how he ended up on Dash's bad side, but the broody prince sure is hot when he gets mad.

Dash has worked long and hard to play Prince Justice at Fairyland. Now, instead of focusing on his own performance, he is forced to train newbie Nate to be the perfect prince. Nate's annoying ease with the guests coupled with his charm and good looks could dethrone Dash from his number one spot ... so why does he secretly want to kiss him?

Fairyland heats up as sparks fly between the two rival princes. Will they get their fairytale romance before they're kicked out of Fairyland for good?

Find out in this standalone MM contemporary romance by Jaxon Knight, set in an amusement park where fairytales can come true.

ALSO PUBLISHED BY GREY KELPIE STUDIO

Mischief and Mayhem by Jaxon Knight

Mischief

Protecting royalty at Fairyland theme park seemed about as far from Afghanistan as Cody could get. But the hot new rollercoaster brings up some unexpected trouble - and not the kind of trouble he knows how to handle alone.

Mayhem

Dean loves running the Spaceship Mayhem roller coaster - he gets to meet new people every day! When he sees a handsome, troubled security guard repeatedly fail to ride it, he sees an opportunity to help. And maybe they can be more than friends?

Cody reluctantly accepts cute, boy-next-door Dean's help and sparks fly between them, but between mischief, mayhem and miscommunication, can they ever make a relationship work?

Mischief and Mayhem is a slow burn, opposites attract MM sweet romance featuring snark, foolishness, motorbikes, assumptions, the chicken door and a HEA

Recipe for Chaos by Jaxon Knight

The recipe is simple:

    Charlie cooks an amazing meal

    Charlie impresses heir to the theme park Max Jones

    Charlie gets a promotion and a dash of control over his
kitchen

But the perfect recipe becomes unpalatable with one wrong
ingredient and Max Jones is not behaving how Charlie
expected...

Max is meant to inherit the entire Fairyland theme park but he
just wants to party, have fun and bed as many people as possible.
That is, until he meets Charlie and falls for him so hard he can't
even finish the delicious meal.

Charlie doesn't have time for clubs or helicopter flights over the city, but Max is accustomed to getting what he wants, and he wants Charlie.

Featuring one part Billionaire, one part sensible chef, six cups of attraction, a generous dose of snark and a freshly prepared Happy Ever After.

Made in United States
North Haven, CT
14 April 2023

35415091R00146